THE
HUMAN
CONDITION

Also by
Will Overby

August

Drum

For Kids:

The Movie House Mystery

The Lost Treasure of Kilimanjaro

The Mummy's Tomb

The River of Gold

THE

HUMAN

CONDITION

Short Fiction and Poetry

WILL OVERBY

BLACK CAT BOOKS

DAWSON SPRINGS, KENTUCKY
2013

This is a work of fiction. Names, characters, businesses, places, events and incidents are either the products of the author's imagination or used in a fictitious manner. Any resemblance to actual persons, living or dead, or actual events is purely coincidental.

"October Sunday Morning" originally appeared in the
Spring 1992 issue of Gadfly
Published by Madisonville Community College/University of Kentucky

ISBN-13: 978-0615792040
ISBN-10: 0615792049

CONTENTS

Stories

The majority of this collection of stories comes from the late 1980s and early 1990s when I was struggling to develop my voice as a writer. Short stories were never my thing. I just never felt I could say all I wanted in so few words. As a result, in those early days I started many novels that never got past the first chapter or so. Some of them, as you will see, found new life as short stories; others were mercifully abandoned. What follows here are the best of the best that survived.

Burying the Dead

I passed by a house for several years where I would occasionally see a young woman sitting on the porch in a wheelchair. I began weaving a story around her and how she came to be paralyzed. One summer she was just no longer there. I never found out who she was or whatever happened to her. It's haunted me ever since.

Jo sits by the living room window, watching the cars rush by against the barren winter landscape. Behind her, the floor furnace bangs and pops. She detests winter. She has ever since the accident. The cold makes her joints ache fiercely.

She unlocks her brake and rolls the wheelchair into the kitchen. Hot spiced tea will be good. She finds a clean mug in the dish drainer and turns the flame on beneath the kettle. Outside, the snow has begun to fall again. She can see it between the kitchen curtains, but she is ignoring it. She refuses to be frightened of it today.

* * *

Jo was once engaged to Gary. Gary was kind and decent—a good man. He was a farmer, like Jo's father, and they had planned to buy twenty acres on Bald Knob Road and build a house and live there the rest of their lives.

But one snowy January evening they were returning from the movies in Springfield. Gary's car hit a patch of ice and he lost control. They hit a Ford pickup head-on. Gary's head broke both the steering wheel and the windshield. He was killed instantly. Jo's spine was broken, paralyzing her from the waist down. The driver of the truck—Harvey Parker—emerged without a scratch. It wasn't fair. Harvey was an old man and Gary was barely twenty. Harvey should have been the one to die; he was not even wearing a seatbelt.

The movie they had gone to see was *The Breakfast Club* with Molly Ringwald and Judd Nelson. Odd that she still remembers that.

* * *

The kettle screams for her attention, and she shuts it off, then pours the steaming water into her mug—the one with Garfield saying "This is *MY* mug!"—and stirs in the tea mix, watching it dissolve.

She sits silent and still, sipping her tea. She would like to move closer to the furnace, but it would be difficult to maneuver her chair now without spilling her cup. She drains the mug and swirls the remaining undissolved tea granules. If she were a fortune teller, like Madame Rosa, maybe she would be able to read the granules and see her future.

Shortly before the accident, she and Gary stopped by Madame Rosa's modest house on Seventh Street for fun. "Let's see what she says," Gary laughed. "Let's see if we'll be millionaires by the time we're thirty."

Madame Rosa's home was intimate and immaculate, like the home of an old spinster—not what Jo expected. She thought it would be full of red velvet chairs and hurricane lamps and odd antiques. Madame Rosa seated them at a small desk in one corner of the parlor. A hand-lettered sign propped against a banker's lamp said:

Fortunes Told
$10.00

Gary slid two fives across the desk and Madame Rosa, a thin pale woman with a hawk nose and sharp piercing eyes, tucked the bills into a cigar box. She took Jo's palm and studied the lines and curves and wrinkles, her brow knitted in concentration. "I see a long life," she said finally. That was it. No other adjectives. Jo has wondered about that ever since. Madame Rosa said nothing about a good life or a tormented one, just a long one.

Madame Rosa reached out for Gary's hand. "I'll do yours at no extra charge," she told him. Gary smiled at Joe and turned up his palm for the old woman. Madame Rosa looked at it, then back into Gary's eyes. "You have had a good life, yes?"

Gary nodded. "Yeah. Sure."

"A happy life?"

"Yeah."

She let go of his hand. "You are going away," she said. "You will leave all you love."

Gary laughed nervously. "Where am I going?"

Madame Rosa blinked. "I don't know."

On the way home that night Gary called Madame Rosa's act a bunch of shit and a waste of ten dollars. A week later he was dead.

* * *

The light outside has become soft and purple. Jo rolls up to the front door and peers through the curtains. The snow is still coming down, fast and thick. The edge of the porch is covered.

In the summer Jo likes to sit on the porch and feel the velvet breeze on her face. The summer is the only time her legs do not hurt. The cats like the porch in summer also. The two of them sit outside the door and meow for her to come out, then they jump into her lap and sit contentedly until she goes back inside.

But the cats are not there today. More than likely they have bedded down somewhere in the barn.

Mom and Dad still have not come back from shopping in town. Jo looks at the road, at the wisps of snow blowing across the blacktop, and wishes they would drive up soon.

* * *

A quarter of a mile down the road from where Jo lives is Miller Cemetery. Gary is buried there. If she parts the living room curtains and cranes her neck, she can almost see the entrance sign. It comforts her to know he is so close.

Sometimes in warm weather, Jo persuades her father to drive her down by Gary's grave. The marker is simple:

GARY WAYNE ADAMS
1964 – 1985

She rarely cries anymore when she sees it, but the drive to the cemetery usually depresses her for days.

The last time her father took her, back in late October, he said, "When are you gonna let him rest, Jo?"

She looked at him, tears of hurt stinging her eyes. But he wouldn't look back at her. "He's *dead*, Jo. You're wasting your whole life pining over a dead man."

Back at home she tried to seek comfort by reading in her bible, but the first verses she came to was a passage in Luke:

> *And he said unto another, Follow me. But he said, Lord, suffer me first to go and bury my father.*
>
> *Jesus said unto him, Let the dead bury their dead; but go thou and preach the kingdom of God.*

Since then, theses verses have always bothered her. She can't believe that Jesus would be so callous about a man's dead father. And sometimes as she lies awake at night, with the winter wind whistling around the corners of the house, the words come back to her: *Let the dead bury their dead. . .*

* * *

Jo rolls into her bedroom and swings open the closet door. With some difficulty, she manages to pull down her winter coat and tug it around her. She takes a look about the room—her narrow bed, the bare walls, the dusty drapes—then pushes herself out into the hall.

At the front door she stops for a moment, her heart pounding. *Why am I doing this?* She buries the thought and opens the door, catching her breath. The world is white. She rolls out onto the porch and the stabbing wind lashes at her cheeks. Snowflakes land and melt on her eyelashes and in her hair; she wishes she had brought her wool tam.

The ramp down to the yard is covered in snow, of course. She looks at it for a moment, then angles her chair and starts down it. Halfway to the yard, the wheels slip and she feels herself going sideways. She envisions herself lying helpless and half-frozen in the snow, waiting and freezing until her parents come back. But she ignores the panic and slowly makes her way down to the end of the ramp.

Now, sitting in the yard, she looks toward the gravel drive. She can barely see its edges outlined by wispy brown grass that pushes up stubbornly through the new snow. She pulls in a cold stinging breath and pushes at the wheels, moving toward the line of grass. The chair feels twenty times heavier than usual, and Jo is reminded of the time last summer when she bogged down in the mud. But that was different; that time her father had been there to push her out.

By the time she feels the gravel crunch beneath the front wheels her body is coated in a layer of sweat. She is exhausted. Her fingers are red and tingling from holding the snow-coated wheels; she wishes she had brought gloves.

The road is only fifty feet in front of her. She starts toward it. The chair moves more easily on the packed gravel.

And suddenly, she is on the road. The thought comes again: *Why am I doing this?* A whispery sound reaches her ears, and she realizes it is a car coming toward her on the opposite side. *Please don't let them stop. Please God. . .*

The car, a red Buick with its headlights on bright, sails past her, it occupants staring at her as they go by. But the car does not even slow down. It bathes her with a splash of ice and slush. She wipes the cold wet from her face and pushes onward. In a few minutes she has reached the turnoff into the cemetery. She is surprised as how quickly she made it.

The drive of the cemetery is gravel, just like the drive at home, but it is bumpier. It takes all her strength to keep the chair going straight over the larger rocks. The snowflakes are larger and faster now. Jo looks back and realizes she cannot even see the blue siding of the house. Ahead of her is Gary's gravestone, half-covered in white. She tosses a strand of sweaty, wet hair from her eyes. The cold air feels good. Her fingers are almost completely numb, but she forces her hands to grip the wheels and push, grip the wheels and push, grip the wheels and push. . .

(1991)

A Cold Day in March

This was a very personal story for me. I'll leave it at that.

I was fourteen years old when I learned the truth about my grandfather.

Spring was late that year. I remember because I was wearing a scratchy wool sweater and faded corduroys when I came bounding down the stairs for breakfast. Late as usual.

At first everything appeared the same: the aroma of coffee and bacon clung heavily to the air; my sister, Ellie, a full head taller than I and twice as strong, sat hunched over a bowl of oatmeal and a tattered copy of Jane Eyre; the radio in the corner blared to no one in particular, giving us the latest on Ike and the Soviets and the Suez; my mother stood at the counter, packing roast beef sandwiches into our shiny lunch boxes and filling our Thermos bottles with milk. But something was different, so shockingly different that it took me a moment to realize what was out of place: Dad wasn't there.

My father was always the first awake. It was he who stumbled downstairs in the dark to start the percolator and listen to the news. He had never failed to be seated in his place with the morning paper when I came in for breakfast. But this morning, the *Times* was still folded, lying beside a half-finished cup of coffee.

"Where's Dad?" I asked. Ellie looked up, and Mother visibly jumped. Something was wrong.

Mother turned a pale, strained face to me. "Sit down, John." I did as I was told, my heart pounding. Was he hurt? Dead? Mother pulled out her chair and fell into it. "There's something I have to tell you. Your father should have done it years ago, but he's. . . not able to at the moment."

I could contain myself no longer. "Is he all right? Is he hurt?"

"He's all right. He's resting. He's in the den." She swallowed. "Please don't be angry with him when I tell you this. You don't know how hard it's been on him— on us—all these years."

"What?"

"We just found out this morning that his father— your grandfather—died yesterday."

I was stunned. "That's crazy. He's been dead for years, since before I was born."

Mother was shaking her head. "He's always been alive."

"I don't understand." I glanced at Ellie. "Did you

know about this?

"Not 'til this morning." She turned down the corner of the page to mark her place and set the book down.

I looked back at Mother. "But why did you lie to us all this time?"

"Try to understand," Mother said, her voice becoming defensive and high-pitched. "It wasn't really a lie. We hadn't heard from him in so long. . . He came to see us right after Ellie was born, and that's the last contact we'd had with him. He'd married again a few years before and he and his wife had a son, although your father has never met him."

Ellie and I both knew this much. My father's parents had divorced when he'd been very young—a scandalous thing in the 1920s. After the death of his mother, he'd gone to live with an aunt, while his father had caroused and traveled and hadn't seen him very much.

I was shaking my head. "I still don't understand. Why lie to us all this time?"

Mother shrugged. "I asked myself that many times. Your father always said he thought it best, that both of you would be better off thinking your grandfather dead than knowing he refused to have anything to do with us." She leaned forward, lowering her voice to a whisper. "I don't think it was your grandfather at all."

"What do you mean?" Ellie asked.

"I don't think your father wanted a relationship because of the way he was treated as a child. I think he saw it as a sort of punishment for the man who neglected him all those years ago." She sighed. "Anyway, when Naomi—"

"Who?"

"Your father's stepmother. When she called to tell

us this morning, your father. . . went to the den."

I rose from the table. "I'm going in to talk to him."

"No, John," Mother said, holding up one hand like a crossing guard. "He's had a bad morning. The last thing he needs is for you to go in there and be angry with him."

I looked at her. This was absurd. I wasn't angry or anything even close to it. I was confused. I had just been bombarded with information my fourteen-year-old mind refused to accept. I just wanted to talk with Dad so that maybe I could understand a little more. I wanted to put all that into words, but there seemed to be a gap between my brain and my lips. Instead, I merely looked at Mother and mumbled, "I won't be angry."

I heard her call after me, but I left the kitchen and passed through the dark hallway to the closed door of the den. Inside, I could hear Beethoven playing softly on the hi-fi—the Ninth Symphony. I knocked gently. "Dad?" There was no answer, so I eased the door open slightly.

He lay on the sofa, still in his robe and pajamas, one hand across his chest and the other holding an open bottle of scotch. His eyes were closed as if he were asleep. I started to back out, but his hoarse slurred voice stopped me. "Don't go. C'm'ere for a minute."

I stepped back into the den and eased myself down on the sofa beside his slippered feet. "Mother just told me," I said. "I'm sorry about. . ."

"No need to be sorry." He leaned over and capped the bottle, set it on the floor. "I'm the one who should be sorry, denying you your grandfather all these years." He sat up and rubbed his hands over his face. I watched him, fascinated as a scientist studying some new breed of insect. The lines beneath his eyes seemed deeper, his jaw slacker, and his short hair seemed woven with a few new strands of silver. I had never seen my father look so old, and it frightened me.

Suddenly, I realized he had been crying. "I can't believe I feel this way," he said as he wiped his eyes. "I never thought I would be sad when he died. Never. I guess I'm not crying over what was, but over the way things could have been, the relationship with him I always wanted but never had." He put an arm around my shoulders. "I tried so hard to not be like him. I always tried to be there for you."

"You were, Dad, you were," I told him, although I know now that he was talking more for himself rather than me.

He looked at me with red eyes. "Would you do a big favor for your old man?"

"Anything."

"Will you go to the funeral with me today?"

I suddenly realized how much my father wanted me to say yes, how much he was depending on me and how deeply he respected me, almost as if I were the parent and he the child. "I'll go if you want me to."

"You don't have to, you know."

"I know."

"Your mother doesn't want to, and I'd rather not ask Ellie. Neither of them likes funerals. I don't want to go by myself—"

"Dad, I'll go. I don't mind."

He patted my shoulder and smiled crookedly. "Thank you, John."

* * *

That afternoon, dressed in our best suits, the two of us loaded into the Ford and headed out of town. The sun was bright, but the warmth seemed to not reach us, as if some invisible shield were filtering the rays. I shivered, wishing I had brought an overcoat.

I reached down and flipped on the radio. Frankie Lymon and the Teenagers came blaring out. Dad glanced at me. "Please, John. Not today." He turned it off, leaving us in gloomy silence once more.

I looked at him out of the corner of my eye. His hat was slightly askew and his tie crooked. His knuckles were white around the steering wheel, the way they had been the time we rode the roller coaster at Cedar Point Park. His closely-cropped mustache twitched every now and then like a dying wasp. "Don't worry," I told him. "It'll be all right."

"Do I look worried?"

I nodded. "Yes." He glanced at me, and I looked back at the barren winter landscape we were passing. "You haven't even told me where we're going."

"Cedar Hill."

"That's only an hour's drive."

"I know."

"You mean he only lived an hour away and you two never saw each other?"

"Yes."

"I don't understand why you never tried to contact him. It looks like—"

"For God's sake, John, you're not making this any easier."

"I'm sorry."

"Just. . . please be quiet."

* * *

A little while later we came to a stop on the side of a street in Cedar Hill. The funeral home had once been a fine brick mansion, and the builder's Southern heritage was evident in the Greek-columned portico and the fanlight windows above the doorways. I shivered. I couldn't imagine anyone living here.

We stepped out of the car, and Dad let me straighten his tie, then we headed for the front door. He had put an arm around my shoulders again, gripping me so tightly I thought I might have a bruise. He sighed deeply, his breath fogging the window of the door, then ushered me inside.

The moist heat inside the foyer seemed to blast against my face, and the overpowering stench of flowers was nearly suffocating. Dad pulled off his hat and hung it on the coat rack, then bent to sign the register, his hands shaking.

The funeral director appeared, looking like another corpse, arms crossed before himself like a bodyguard. "Are you here for the Gregory funeral?" My father nodded, and the director showed us the way with a great sweep of his arm.

We stood forever in the back of the chapel, Dad behind me, his fingers biting into my shoulders like claws. We began to move forward, inching our way toward the copper-colored casket lit on either side by pink hurricane floor lamps. A number of people sat about the room on the creaky wooded chairs, and now as we entered, they began to whisper. I heard one old woman say clearly, "That's his other son, Thomas. Must be his boy with him."

I looked at the floor as we neared the front of the chapel, not wanting to see the dead face. I didn't know why I was so nervous, since I hadn't known this man. I suppose that knowing we were related, knowing how he had treated my father, and knowing that Dad was so disturbed all had enveloped me in a fog. My steps were almost numb with apprehension, as if I were walking on a sponge.

An overweight, sixtyish woman in a stiff, black dress suddenly appeared before us. Her hair had been haphazardly rolled, and her eyes were red and wet. She captured my father with her flabby arms and engulfed him into her massive frame. "Thomas! I'm so glad you came." Fresh tears began to roll down her round face. "He's gone now, he's gone now," she said, and it would not be the last time that day she would repeat it. "He's not suffering now."

My father pulled away from her. "How are you holding up, Naomi?" he asked in a dry voice.

"Well as can be expected, I guess." Her gaze fell on me. "Is this your son?"

"Yes. This is John."

She smiled and extended her hand to me. "Hi, John. You never did get to meet me or your grandfather, did you?"

"No, ma'am."

"That's a shame. I know he would've been proud of you." In the silence that followed, I thought how strange it was for her to say that.

And then we began to move toward the casket. I watched the scuffed toes of my shoes as I walked, my heart pounding like a sledgehammer.

And then we were looking at him. He was just an old man lying there, sort of nondescript, really. Except. . . except he looked like Dad. The nose. The slant of the eyes. He even wore a mustache like Dad's. It was all unnerving. Thirty years later, when we would bury my father, I would look into the casket and shiver so violently that my wife would ask me if I needed to go back home.

But for now, we were all three standing in the funeral home in Cedar Hill. Dad began to wipe his eyes with a wadded handkerchief. "He looks nice, Naomi."

A young man came up behind us and touched Naomi on the shoulder. "Mother, we've still got two hours until the funeral. Do you care if I go down to the coffee shop for a little while?"

There was no mistaking who this was. I had seen him a hundred times in a faded photograph in our family album. Except in the picture he was three years old.

"Just a minute," Naomi said. She took hold of my father's hand. "Thomas," she said to him, "this is your brother, Stephen."

They looked at each other for a very awkward moment and then, hesitantly, shook hands. "I'm very glad at last to meet you," Stephen said.

"Same here," Dad said, barely audible.

"I just wish it were under better circumstances."

"Right."

Naomi pointed to me. "This is Thomas' son, umm. . ."

"John," I said, shaking Stephen's hand.

"Hello, John." He turned back to Dad. "I was just going to go down the street for some coffee. Would you two like to join me?"

My father looked back at the casket. "Well. . ."

"We have a lot of catching up to do."

"Go ahead," Naomi said. "I'll be fine."

Dad took a deep breath. "All right."

Stephen smiled. "Good. Let me get my coat."

* * *

A few minutes later we were sitting at a tiny table in the drafty restaurant down the street. Dad spilled the sugar and tried not to let us see his hands shake as he wiped it up.

Stephen blew on his steaming coffee. "So what do you do, Thomas?"

"I manage a radio station. WSPG in Springfield."

Stephen's eyes widened. "That's the one with the big rock and roll show every Friday night, isn't it?"

Dad nodded and took a sip from his cup. "Right. I don't care too much for that music myself, but it seems to be very popular."

"Like it or not, I think it's here for good."

"How old are you now?"

"Twenty-one."

"What do you do?"

"I'm still in college right now. I graduate in May. Journalism. I had my internship at the Times, and I'll go to work there full-time in June."

Dad nodded. "I wasn't able to go to college. I had no money. And then there was the war."

"Oh, yes, the war." Stephen smiled. "Well, maybe all that's behind us now." He raised his cup to his lips, then set it back down. "How'd you get your radio job?"

Dad laughed humorlessly. "Just sheer luck. I got some radio experience during the war, and when I came back home, the station needed someone. I was a jockey for a long time before I moved up."

"Radio must be exciting."

Dad's eyes were narrow over the rim of his cup. "It's all right."

Stephen glanced at me, then back at Dad. "You have any other children?"

"A daughter. Ellie. She's fifteen, a year older than John."

"What's your wife's name?"

Dad looked at the table for a moment. "Mary."

"That's a nice name. Is she pretty?"

"I think so."

"So what does she look like? You got her picture?"

Dad looked up suddenly, slamming his fist down on the table and sloshing coffee out of his cup. "What's your game?"

Stephen looked at him, an astonished look coming across his features. "No game. I'm just trying to get to know my big brother."

"Yeah?" Dad took a paper napkin and began wiping up the spilled coffee. "I think I can do without it myself."

Stephen was suddenly angry. "What's wrong with you, Thomas? I just asked you a few questions. We are brothers, after all. Just because we've never met—"

"Exactly," Dad said. "We've never met. But just because we're brothers doesn't mean I have to tell you every single damn thing about my life."

"Sorry."

"Yeah, well, maybe this wasn't such a good idea." Dad bent over the table, rubbing his eyes with his hand. "I shouldn't've come, I shouldn't've come to the funeral."

"How can you say that, Thomas? He was your father, after all."

Dad looked at him icily. "Well, that never seemed to mean very much to him." He swallowed. "I'm sorry. I didn't mean to lash out at you like that."

"It's all right."

"No. It's not." Dad swiped a hand through his hair. "You must think I'm. . . crazy."

"We're all a little crazy right now."

"I must've thought about our meeting a thousand times. And every time it crossed my mind, I came up with all kinds of things to say to you." He stopped.

"Like what?" Stephen asked.

Dad sighed. "Like how I resented you and was so jealous of you because you were able to grow up with a father—my father. He taught you things and spent time with you and was there for you. And he never gave a damn about me."

"That's not true."

"Of course it is."

"He did care about you, Thomas. He may not have been able to show it, but he did care. He was always talking about you, about things you did. Always comparing me to you. I hated you sometimes because I felt like I could never measure up."

"Really?" Dad laughed bitterly. "It's funny, isn't it? We never knew each other, yet we hated one another." He looked at his watch. "We should probably get back and be with Naomi."

Stephen toyed with the salt dispenser. "Thomas. . ."

"Yes?"

"I'm glad we could talk like this."

"Me, too," Dad said. "Me, too."

(1990)

3rd Ave

"3rd Ave" was written in the fall of 1989 for submission to that year's Playboy *college fiction contest. It's the only story I can think of that I wrote with a specific purpose in mind. I didn't win.*

Doc had been living in the basement of the house on Third Avenue for three weeks when he found the boy. Actually, the boy found *him*.

Doc was returning from his usual morning probe of the garbage cans in the back alley when he saw a flash of blue in the cellar door. Those damned kids again. They were always breaking into the upstairs of the house. Glittery splinters of crushed crack vials and gooey used condoms were the testaments of the coming and going. In the daylight, Doc had no qualms about running the little bastards off. The night was different. In darkness, when he heard the tell-tale crash and tumble above, he would barricade himself into the sleep-corner, trying not to breathe lest they hear him. He would sit forever in one position, sometimes for a couple of hours, the cold from the concrete floor seeping achingly up through his buttocks, while footsteps clamored above, coupled with hoots and shouts.

Rarely did anyone venture downstairs. Since the house was huge, most of the invaders were content to ramble through the top three floors. But also, the cellar door was hidden in a shadowy alcove, so hardly any of the trespassers ever saw it. That was why, when Doc entered the hallway and found the door open, he was shocked to see the boy disappear down the stairs.

He dropped his bag of goods and peered cautiously down into the darkness. "You better come out of there," he said, and the gruff sound of his own voice surprised him. There was no response. "I'm warning you."

Something toppled over and hit the floor with a muffled thud. "Damn you," Doc whispered. He swiped a hand through his greasy mop of dark hair. "Look kid—whoever you are. I don't wanna hurt you. I just want you to leave, okay? Just get the hell out, and I won't touch you. Okay?"

Doc inched his way down into the dark silence. In the dim light he could see that the kid had knocked over one of the stacks of boxes that served as a wall for one of Doc's rooms. "Shit."

A hand shot out between the steps and grabbed one of his ankles. If he hadn't been gripping the rickety banister he would have plummeted down to the concrete floor, more than likely breaking his neck. As it was, he merely toppled forward, landing shoulder-first on the steps. Knife-like pain blinded him for a moment. "You little fuck!" he screamed through clenched teeth. "You coulda killed me!" His fingers inched their way beneath his flannel shirt to feel his shoulder. The skin was already swollen, but he could detect no broken bones. He swiped his coat sleeve across his chapped lips and was surprised to see blood on it. He had bitten his tongue in the fall. He leaned over and spat.

The boy was still crouching behind the steps, looking at him with round, frightened eyes. Now that his vision had adjusted to the dark, Doc could see the boy was dirty and ragged. A fresh scab ran beneath one eye. The coat he was wearing was paper-thin, and the fringes from the ratty cuffs hung down like spaghetti. He was wearing a pair of Nikes at least two sizes too big for him; the top was worn out of one, and Doc could see the kid's dirty black toes.

"What do you want?" Doc asked him, and the boy hunkered down. For one aching moment, Doc thought he looked amazingly like his own son. But that was impossible—Danny was in school in California. Living with Ellen. God. All of that seemed like a dream now.

The boy moved into a corner. Doc's eyes searched him out in the dark. "Look, if you want money, I don't have any."

A voice, shrill and thin, came back to him: "Blow ya, mister."

"What?"

"Blow ya for five dollars."

Doc caught the boy's gaze. The kid looked back at him, serious and unblinking. Doc's mouth had gone dry. He thought of the plastic bag upstairs. "You want some food?"

The boy nodded, his eyes growing large.

"C'mon. I've got some stuff."

The boy emerged from the dark corner and followed Doc up the stairs. Just as they reached the cellar door, something crashed outside, followed by tramping feet and loud jovial voices. Doc motioned for the boy to halt, then silently shut the door and barricaded it with a two-by-four. "Back down," he whispered. The voices were adult, three or four of them, and while he knew he could scare off a bunch of kids, grown men were a different matter.

"What is it?" the boy asked.

"Some people. We gotta hide."

He led the boy to the sleep-corner and took to the well-practiced task of sealing them off from the rest of the cellar by sliding a wall of heavy boxes of junk across the opening. Now they were entombed in a cubicle no bigger than three feet by five feet.

"You want me to blow you now?"

"Shut up. They'll hear you."

Upstairs the thudding steps and voices continued, sometimes quieter as the vandals moved to the upper levels of the house. Doc sat like a stone, praying no one would find the cellar. But suddenly, someone was pounding on the door, and Doc's heart jumped in his chest.

"Whad'ya doin'?" someone hollered.

"Door's locked, man."

"Come on, they're leavin'."

Doc and the boy sat in silence as the footsteps faded. The boy started to get up, but Doc stopped him. "Let's wait a few more minutes."

When he was sure no one was left in the house, they ventured out and climbed up the steps. The motherfuckers had taken his food. "We'll have to go out and find something to eat," he said.

"I know a good place."

"You do?"

"Yeah. There's a place not far from here."

On their way out, Doc caught sight of something in one of the rooms. One of the vandals had spray-painted the walls. Among the usual vulgarities was written "ELLEN IS A BITCH," and Doc laughed in spite of himself.

Outside, the boy looked at him. "Why were you laughin' back there?"

Doc told him about the graffiti, then said, "My wife's name was Ellen, and she *was* a bitch."

"Where is she now?"

"In L.A. With our son."

"How old is he?"

"Thirteen." He looked down at the boy. "How old are you?"

"Ten."

"What's your name?"

"Jones."

"Nice to meet you, Jones. I'm Doc." He extended his hand and the boy shook it.

"Are you really a doctor?"

"I was once. Long story. Pharmaceuticals were involved, and I lost my license and got sent to prison for a few months. Then Ellen and Danny left. Then I lost my house." He stopped and looked down at the boy. "Where's your parents, Jones?"

He shrugged. "I don't remember. I was livin' with my aunt. Been there since I was a little kid."

"What happened?"

"I ran away. She was mean. Used to lock me in the

closet. She wouldn't even let me go to the bathroom. Then when I couldn't hold it any longer, when I'd piss myself, she'd whip me for it. So I got outa there." He licked his lips. "But I can make it on my own. I have since last spring. I get enough hustlin' I can buy food."

"Is that what you do? Hustle?"

"Yeah."

"But you don't like it, surely."

Jones looked at him, then quickly shifted his gaze. "What do you think? I'm no faggot, but I gotta eat." He stopped and pointed. "There it is."

Doc squinted in the bright sun. Fountain Place. An outdoor shopping mall. He remembered it well from coming here with Ellen. Lots of good restaurants in Fountain Place.

"C'mon." Jones bounded across the intersection and headed for the back of the line of buildings. Doc followed, glancing around cautiously.

With luck, they found the garbage cans of Sarducci's, what had once been Doc's favorite restaurant, and pulled out several decent scraps. Back at the house, he and Jones dined on the remains of filet mignon and pecan pie.

Jones looked up, a smear of steak sauce on his chin. "I know where you can get a mattress."

The boy led him to a junk pile just a few blocks away. Sure enough, someone had disposed of a perfectly good Beauty Rest. Though stained and reeking of beer and urine, it was solid enough, and it would at least be better than sleeping on cold concrete.

Jones helped him carry it back to the house, and on the way Doc caught sight of the two of them reflected in a store-front window—an urchin that looked like something from Dickens and a forty-year-old man with a graying beard wearing a threadbare Brooks Brothers suit and L.L. Bean hunting shoes. He looked away, feeling as if he'd been caught spying on someone else.

The next day, after Doc had slept soundly on the new bed, Jones woke him and presented him with a cup of hot coffee. "Where did you get this?" Doc asked, thankful for the heat as he huddled over the steaming cup.

"At a coffee stand."

"But didn't you have to pay. . . ?" He stopped in mid-sentence and took a sip, eyeing the boy. "Did you hustle last night?"

Jones shrugged.

"Why? You don't have to do that anymore. You can stay with me. We can find enough food without—"

"Save it, okay?" Jones looked more like an old man of seventy than a boy of ten. "I ain't eatin' outa garbage cans all the time, I just ain't. I don't care what you think."

Doc leaned back against the cold wall. "Doesn't it scare you?"

Jones looked at his feet, wiggling his exposed toes. "I need the money." He raised his eyes to Doc. "We both need the money." He ran his tongue across his lips. "I can go out and—and work. I can bring the money to you. You could buy us food. Maybe you could rent us a room—"

"Stop it," Doc said. "Stop it, Jones. I won't let you do this. Not while you're with me. We'll find food. It may not be hot, but it'll keep us alive."

Jones looked down, fingering the stitching on the mattress. "There is another way."

* * *

It was night again. The boy had taken him to Fifth

Street. "I used to live in this neighborhood," Doc said. He pointed toward a neat brick townhouse. "That was mine."

"Shut up," Jones whispered. "Follow me."

The rain had begun just as they left the house on Third Avenue, and now the bone-chilling November drizzle had seeped through their clothes. Doc thought again of the hole in Jones' shoe and shuddered. He turned up his collar and fell into step behind the boy. They huddled in a doorway out of the rain, out of the pools of light thrown by the streetlamps.

"What are we doing?" Doc asked, his breath a large white puff.

Jones craned his neck, peering down the street. "Here comes someone now," he said softly. He drew something out of his pocket and pressed it into Doc's hand.

In the dim light, Doc could see that it was a knife— a child's jackknife with a plastic handle. He opened the stainless-steel blade and found it caked with dried blood. He looked at Jones and his mouth dropped open. "I—I can't," he stammered, sickened.

Jones' voice was cold and steady. "Do it."

Doc looked around. A man with an umbrella was hurriedly making his way down the street toward them.

"Do it," Jones whispered again.

The man passed them and Doc stepped out behind him. He reached out a shaking hand and gripped the man's shoulder.

Startled, the man turned, the streetlamp shining brightly on his face. The frightened eyes behind the tortoise-shell glasses, the slack, open mouth, the clean-shaven jaw—they were all familiar. Doc jumped back, nearly stumbling on the uneven sidewalk. "Frank," he whispered. "Frank. . . "

Frank was squinting at him. Then his eyes flew open wide. "Doc! Doc, is that you?"

Then Jones was screaming. "Do it! Do it!"

Half in panic, half in reflex, Doc plunged the knife home and felt the sudden gush of liquid warmth.

Frank clutched Doc's arm as he sank to the ground. His eyes were still wide, but now with terror and pain. Dock watched him fall, fascinated. The knife fell to the sidewalk with a dull clatter.

Instantly Jones was upon the body, fishing for Frank's wallet. He brought it out and stuffed it into his coat, then searched the other pockets. Doc shrank back into the doorway, his legs weak and quaking, his mouth like sandpaper. He wanted to vomit.

A voice was suddenly shouting. A police car, probably on routine rounds, had pulled up beside them. Spotlights were blazing on.

"C'mon!" Jones screamed at him.

They fled blindly down an alley between buildings, crossed over a fence, and headed down the next street, running for Third Avenue.

He was following a child. He was trusting a damned *child* to get him out of this.

Sirens wailed behind them and Doc could see the whirling red and blue lights one street over.

"Hurry!" Jones screamed. "We're almost there!"

* * *

Back in the safety of the cellar, Jones produced a cigarette lighter. He held it while Doc counted the money from Frank's wallet. "How much is there?"

"Over a hundred dollars," Doc said. His tongue felt thick and slimy in his mouth.

Jones let out a squeal of delight. "We're gonna live

like fuckin' *kings*!"

He was smiling broadly, and Doc could see the rows of stained, rotten teeth in the kid's mouth. Suddenly, he hated the boy. He was revolted by him. Most of all, he was ashamed of what he had let the little asshole talk him into.

Instantly, he was atop Jones, his calloused hands gripping the boy's bony throat. "I should kill you," he spat at him. "I should kill you for this."

Beneath him, Jones said, "Yeah. But you won't."

* * *

In the morning, the boy was gone, and with him, Frank's wallet. Doc stayed at the house all day, but Jones did not return. Neither did he show up the next day. And when he didn't come back after the third day, Doc knew he was gone for good.

One morning, while rooting through the cans behind Sarducci's and hoping insanely to find another filet mignon, he saw Jones in the center of the mall.

The boy was standing beside the dry fountain, talking animatedly to a man in a grubby overcoat. Jones caught Doc's gaze and stared at him. Doc waved. Jones looked away and led the other man toward the far entrance.

"Go on then," Doc whispered, half-jealous, half-relieved. "Go to hell, you little shit."

(1989)

Types You Meet in Truckstops

This story is a rarity in that I have no idea what inspired me to write it, other than knowing these "types" from working third shift as a dishwasher in a diner during college.

When he shuffles in, ragged and tired-looking, she notices him from her dark corner in the restaurant. He is about forty, she guesses. Dark greasy hair curls out from under his red Peterbilt cap. He is a big man, not fat, although it is hard to tell because he is wearing a grimy blue chambray work shirt, untucked, and the sleeves torn off; the loose threads of the armholes dangle around his solid brown shoulder like spider webs. He takes a seat on a stool at the counter, orders a cup of coffee. Drinks it black.

It is two in the morning.

When five minutes have passed, she slides out of her booth and threads her way to where he sits staring at the racks of steaming glasses the busboy has just brought out from the dishwasher. She plops down on the empty stool beside him. "Hi."

He turns and regards her for a moment with soft, brown eyes—deer eyes, she thinks—then turns back to his coffee. "H'lo."

"I noticed you come in," she says. "You a trucker?"

"Yeah."

She paws through her purse, searching for her lipstick. She locates it with her fingers and pulls it out, then brings out a mirror and fixes her lips. "Where you headed?"

He turns and looks at her, then turns his attention back to the racks of glasses. "South."

"No kidding?"

"No kidding."

"That's where I'm headed. How far you going?"

He sighs. "Look, missy, I'm married. I don't know what you want, but you're not getting it from me."

Rage clouds her face. "I don't want nothing but a ride. Just a ride south."

"I don't take passengers."

"I don't know what you think I want, but a ride's all I was asking for." She clears her throat. "Guess you thought I was a whore."

"I didn't think no such thing," he says, still staring straight ahead. "It's just that you meet all kinds of people in truckstops, and I make it my policy to not take riders."

She orders a cup of coffee, even though she knows she'll barely have the money to pay for it. While waiting, she says, "I know what you mean about the people you meet. I think I've been to every truckstop between here and Philadelphia—that's where I'm from, Philadelphia. Seen a lot of people I wouldn't want to get next to, if you know what I mean."

He nods. "Said you were headed south. What's in the south?"

"Florida," she says hungrily. "I got an old friend that lives in Tampa. He told me there's all kinds of jobs down there. Said I could get one without any trouble at all."

"Old boyfriend?"

"Yeah," she says, and he nods. "But that's another story."

"How old are you, anyway?"

"Twenty-two."

"Twenty-two. . . " He rubs a hand over his scruffy face. "Jesus."

She looks at him. "What? What about twenty-two?"

He laughs. "I got a daughter your age."

Somehow, his saying this makes her feel better about him. She feels protected, comfortable. She edges closer to him. "What's she like?"

He smiles, still looking straight ahead. "She's got blonde hair, blue eyes, turned-up nose . . . She's got a little scar right below her bottom lip"—he touches a finger lightly to his stubbled chin—"right here, where she fell when she was a baby. Broke her bottle and cut herself." His eyes have gone cloudy, as if he is no longer seeing the shocking fluorescent whiteness of the restaurant. "She's a senior in college. Michigan State."

"What's her name?" she asks, sipping her coffee.

"Karen," he says. "Karen Anne. She's gonna be a teacher. High school."

She is shaking her head. "I couldn't do that. I hate kids."

"I understand," he says. "What's your name, missy?"

She takes another sip of coffee. "Candy."

He extends his hand to her and she takes it. He smiles. "I'm Carl."

There is a painting on the wall—oil on black velvet—of a truck speeding down a dark highway. Above it, Christ is peering down from the clouds, pointing the way. "I don't like that picture," she says. "It's creepy."

"I've seen that before, he says. "S'posed to be Jesus protecting the truckers."

She shivers, still looking at it. "Gives me the creeps."

He stretches and glances at his watch. "Jesus," he says. "I gotta go." He pulls a five out of his wallet and tosses it on the counter. "This'll cover yours, too," he tells her.

"Thank you."

He pushes himself off the stool and yawns broadly. "Nice meeting ya," he says.

For a brief instant, she feels desperation clawing its way up her gut. She wants to grab onto him, to keep him here with her, to keep him in her sight. She wants to cling to him, to feel him inside her, to lie beneath the weight of him. She wants to wake in the morning to his steady breathing, then kiss him softly until his eyes open and he wants to make love to her again. She reaches out and touches the back of his hand. "You. . . you sure you don't want some company?" she asks. "Just for tonight?"

He smiles at her, a sad and disappointed smile, and says, "I'm sure." He turns to go, then looks back at her. "Good luck, missy—Candy."

She watches as he disappears through the door, then she makes her way back to the dark booth in the corner and lights a stale cigarette.

* * *

He steps through the glass doors, and she notices him at once. He is young, maybe thirty, blond and bearded, with large hands and narrow, close-set eyes. He is rumpled and tired-looking. He slides into one ancient booth and orders a breakfast plate, then lights a Marlboro and sits staring out the window at the cold, wet, early darkness.

It is three in the morning.

After five minutes, she slips from her seat, pulls out a cigarette and makes her way to his booth. He looks up as she sits down opposite him, and she can see how blue his sleepy eyes are. The smell coming off him is sweat and diesel fuel and Brut aftershave, and his long-sleeve green shirt is unbuttoned at the cuffs and the neck, where blond hair sprouts like the fine down on a baby's head.

"Hi," she says, waving her cigarette. "Got a light?"

(1990)

Two Sketches

These short pieces were part of what I envisioned as a book of character sketches, similar to Spoon River Anthology *but told by an omniscient narrator.* Joey *was a kid that lived next door to me for a while, and this little essay was an attempt to channel some of what I was feeling at the time.* Katrina *was a girl who went to my church; I remember being fascinated with her eyes and how she seemed to be an old soul in a child's body, and wondering what could have happened in her short life to make her that way.*

Joey

I can be myself with Joey.

The fact that I am twice his age means there is no reason to pretend, to defend myself. I can feel fatherly and vulnerable at the same time. I know of no other person who can milk these strangely marbled emotions from me.

And yet, kind though he is, something about him terrifies me, fills my stomach with raw panic.

Could it be his blatant honesty? He can ask me how much money I earn without even blinking an eye, as if he were an FBI agent. He offers comments and doles out private information the way bankers make small talk at parties: easily, with bravado.

Maybe the terror comes from the fact that he seemingly has no inhibitions. At times I wish that I, like he, could burst out the front door and bound down the steps with a throat-rending, rip-roaring scream, a scream that means nothing more than the joy and satisfaction of being alive at that particular moment. But that would look foolish in a twenty-two-year-old.

It saddens me that he must grow up to learn the realities of adulthood, that he believes the childhood myth that being grown-up is better. But, like everyone else, he will believe, only to learn the truth when he has expended all his childhood energy struggling to become a man.

And maybe what frightens me most is what I see reflected of myself in his eyes. For I know he perceives me as a confused boy/man, caught somewhere between adolescence and manhood, feeling like an ersatz James Dean, knowing I can never go backward to the safe agony of Joey's age, and unsure of how to reach out and grab my future without becoming frozen.

Katrina

Katrina has much to teach me. Maybe it is in the way her eyes betray a maturity far beyond her thirteen years. Or maybe it is in her innocence that seems so pure and genuine. But no matter.

Katrina cares not for the things of childhood and burgeoning adolescence. Her mind is elsewhere. She is yearning to be an adult. Her body is straining and crying to blossom, but her soul is already a full-grown woman.

Look at how she moves. Even though she is trapped in a little girl's body, she has all the grace and style of a prima ballerina. She has only to step across the room to capture my heart.

Why am I so drawn to her?

It must be her eyes—those large, beautiful blue-green eyes that are so old and sad. They speak of endless nights of incomprehensible torture, of terrors both real and imagined that awaken her at night and envelope her in their sinewy grasp. Her eyes are windows, but they are heavily curtained, guarded against peeping-toms such as I.

One day I would like to take her into my arms and kiss her on the forehead like a good father would and console her by telling her the world is not such a bad place. There is much good and happiness if you care to look for it. I would like to tell her I understand her, that I know how it feels to be trapped, to want to break free.

But, strangely, she needs no such talk. She is perfectly calm. If only I could be as she. She seems to know with uncanny patience that all this is temporary. That one day, when her body has caught up with her mind, she will be able to leave all this behind and take flight. And maybe then she will be able to defeat the terrors, to battle them down and stand victorious. But until then, she remains tireless in her endurance, threatened by fear, but undaunted by it.

Yes, Katrina has much to teach me. If I will only be still and listen.

(1989)

Houston's Last Stand

It started innocently enough. The twentieth anniversary of Earth Day had just passed, and everyone was on an environmental kick. I wondered what would happen if one day government regulation went overboard and how random characters from some of my unpublished novels would deal with it. This is as close to science fiction as you'll ever see from me. On a side note, I would never have guessed when I wrote this that I would have a future bank career dealing with—you guessed it—government regulation.

By the time he and Jessie had celebrated their tenth wedding anniversary, just after the New Constitution made the disposal of recyclables a felony, Lee Houston became fed up. His garage, which once housed two cars, now housed a pickup and seven garbage cans—one for each day of the week the sanitation truck ran, and it ran on a schedule everyone but Lee seemed to remember. Jessie had posted the list, clipped from the newspaper, on the garage wall:

MONDAY:	Paper
TUESDAY:	Glass
WEDNESDAY:	Aluminum
THURSDAY:	Plastic
FRIDAY:	Non-Aluminum Metals
SATURDAY:	All Other Recyclables
SUNDAY:	Non-Recyclables and Food Waste

The cans, big green plastic monstrosities on wheels, had been provided by the city, and seven nights a week Lee rolled out the correct can and placed it on the curb. From his driveway he could see one long line of big green plastic cans stretching down Ersatz Drive into infinity. Seven nights a week.

One such night, after wheeling out a load of glass bottles, he came in to find Jessie and their five-year-old son, Corey, sitting in the darkened living room. "Why are you sitting in the dark?"

"We've already used our solar electricity ration for the day," she informed him.

"It's only twenty-thirty."

She shrugged. "Sorry. You know this always happens when you mow the yard. That electric lawn mower really drains our supply."

Lee sank down into his vinyl cotton-shred-stuffed recliner. "Remember when everyone had gas-powered mowers?"

Jessie nodded. "Such a waste of fossil fuels. And the noise! Thank God those are illegal now."

Lee sighed. "But at least you could come in and still have lights at night." He pulled up the tail of his wrinkled cotton shirt and swiped at his sweaty forehead. He looked at the open window where no breeze stirred the curtains. "And at least a guy could turn on some air conditioning and get cool."

Jessie's face contorted in horror. "CFCs!"

"What's air conditioning?" Corey asked.

"Something bad that ate up the ozone. From before the Laws," Jessie told him. "It's one reason you can only play outside for an hour a day, and then only with your sunblock-90."

"Well, be sure and tell him about plastic foam as well," Lee said. "Tell him how we used to go to Burger World and get a big Burger De-Luxe dripping with brown salty grease and sitting in that big foam carton."

Jessie covered Corey's ears. "Please! Not in front of the child. You know the thought of eating beef scares him to death."

"Yes, yes, of course." He stepped into the kitchen to get a drink of water from the new wooden ice box. They'd had it since OCT 2022 when the CFC Law (Environmental Protection Enforcement No. 3,018 [CFC Emitting Devices]) went into effect and the government had come to haul off everyone's refrigerators and air conditioners. He noticed their block of ice inside was decidedly smaller. "When does the ice man come back?" he called to Jessie.

"Friday."

Great. Better savor this cold water now. He lifted the gallon of distilled water and poured a glassful. He drank it slowly, his tongue barely moving to taste something with no taste. "When does the water girl come back?"

"Tomorrow."

"Think she might could bring some Coca-Cola?"

"Lee! You know those are illegal." Jessie clucked her tongue. "Dietary Protection Enforcement No. 746 (Non-Nutritional Foods)."

* * *

The New Constitution, passed by all fifty states, had gone into effect 1 JAN 2021. While including the Bill of Rights from the Old Constitution, the "Healthy Constitution," as it was sometimes called, also incorporated protective laws (or "Enforcements") against things deemed harmful to the human body (by the Surgeon General) and to the environment (by the Environmental Protection Agency).

To Lee, this meant most of the fun things he had once loved were now illegal or gone forever. Even sex was not as enjoyable since the Pill had been recalled with Health Protection Enforcement No. 21 and available birth control methods had been reduced with Sexual Protection Enforcement No. 1,347 (Condoms and Foam).

He knew he was not the only one who felt this way. Sometimes he and some friends from the office would meet in his neighbor's basement for cigars smuggled in all the way from Havana and some bootlegged beer. Once there, they would play cards and talk about the government.

"Just once," Joe DeCanto said, "I wanna go hot-roddin' up the highway in my pickup. Blow that 40-mile-an-hour speed limit all to hell and back. Burn up some gas."

Dan Turner nodded. "And I wanna get a disposable diaper and have my kid shit in it and personally deliver it to that congressman who made the damn things illegal in the first place."

Shane Adams licked his lips. "I wanna put up a grill in my back yard and cook me up a thick juicy T-bone. And I wanna eat it with my fuckin' fingers like some animal. And then I wanna go in the house and get me a beer out of my fridge—a *real* beer, not this fake shit. Gimme a Bud like in the old days."

Lee scratched the red stubble on his chin. "Wonder what they did with all the refrigerators and air conditioners and shit they hauled away?"

Dan grunted. "Prob'ly sent 'em to fuckin' outer space."

Joe took a long draw on his cigar. "I heard they took all that crap and sent it to Third World countries. Sent our goddamned refrigerators and air conditioners to fuckin' *India*."

"Whatever they did," Shane chimed in, "you can bet your ass it's all bein' used somewhere. You know they wouldn't just throw it away. After all," he sneered, "that would be fuckin' *illegal*."

Dan grunted again. "I bet somebody could find out all kinda shit if they could get into that government recyclin' center over at Fort Bush. That's where they take everything. Even the stuff they don't recycle."

Shane turned back to Lee. "What do you think?"

Lee took a swallow of beer from its plastic container. "First, I'd like to plant a bomb in that recycling plant and blow it straight to hell. Then I'd take all those damn big green plastic cans at home, all that paper and glass and aluminum and plastic and tin and garbage, mix it all up in the back of my pickup, and then I'd drive up to Washington and dump it all over the White House lawn."

"All right!" Dan shouted, slapping the table. "Yer

an okay guy."

* * *

But two weeks later, Lee was still thinking about what he'd said. It would be possible, wouldn't it? Storm through those chain-link gates of Fort Bush and throw a bomb in the middle of the government's works. Maybe he could find out if Joe DeCanto had been right—if all those things everyone had been forced to live without had actually been sold to some other country too smart not to use them. He laughed. He'd be arrested, of course. Or killed. Then the second half of his idea would be down the drain. Sorry, no garbage for you, Mr. President.

Maybe he could take someone with him. But who? Dan Turner? No, too slow. Joe Decanto? No, too hot-headed. Now Shane Adams was a possibility—more on Lee's level. And Shane seemed to know where Lee was coming from.

The next evening, Lee went next door and told Shane the plan, told him he was serious. "Are you in?" he asked, fully expecting Shane to say no.

"Hell, yes, I'm in," Shane said.

"Tomorrow night, then. At dark."

* * *

The next morning he locked himself in the garage with the big green plastic cans and a supply of materials he had secured from the hardware store. He knew how to build a bomb; the government had taught him in the Defense Force. He was finished in thirty minutes.

* * *

When the sun was down, Lee pulled his pickup into the garage. He grabbed the first big green plastic can. Newspaper. It fluttered in with a whisper. Next was the rattling of aluminum, then a load of steel food cans.

Then plastic containers tumbled in followed by the glittery crash of glass. He picked up the last big green plastic can. It was mostly full of food waste which was sent to the state farms for compost. He turned the big green plastic can over and the muck dripped in. He stood back and looked at it, at the hodgepodge mixture of garbage in his truck, his heart pounding. The sight of everything mixed together, of banana peels and tin cans and broken glass all stirred up and touching was a mind-blowing rush. He had a hard-on.

There was a light knock on the door and Shane slipped in, pulling a big green plastic can behind him. "I fit everything into one big green plastic can," he said, reeling with bravado. He looked around quickly, as if he thought some government agent might be lurking in the shadows of the garage. "You know, if a cop happened to come in here we'd be arrested on the spot."

"Yep."

Shane turned his big green plastic can up and spilled his garbage into Lee's pickup. He stepped back and stared at it in awe. "Damn, that's a beautiful sight."

Lee nodded. "If there wasn't broken glass in there, I think I'd take off my clothes and get in that mess and roll around in it."

"Fuckin' A."

Lee looked at his watch. "It's almost twenty-one hundred. We'd better get on the road.

* * *

Fort Bush was situated about a hundred kilometers from Lee's hometown. Everyone had received information on it when it had opened. The pamphlets told how much glass, aluminum, plastic, and other material the plant could recycle in one day's time; how energy efficient it was; how much tax money was being saved by it; how much the government was doing for the people and the environment by enacting the sanitation program. And now it was going to be demolished in a split second.

He drove cautiously, obeying every driving enforcement he could remember; he wanted to do nothing to call attention to the little black pickup with a tarp that covered its illegal load. Beside him, Shane was biting his fingernails and twitching his legs. It took them two hours to reach the recycling plant.

Lee parked in a dark grove just off the road about a kilometer from the gates.

"Are we sure we want to do this?" Shane asked, and Lee could tell he was trying to keep his voice from quivering.

Lee looked at him. "Damned right we do. We have a right to know what's going on there."

Shane looked around in terror. "I thought we were just gonna drop the bomb and get out."

"We are. But first I want to see what's going on."

"Shit." Shane ran a hand over his sweaty face. "Maybe I should just stay here. Wait for you."

"Like hell. Don't tell me you just want to sit here and let the government walk on you. Stand up! Fight back!" Lee sighed. "Think about your wife. Think about yourself. Think about having to depend on the government for your power supply. For what you eat. For how you fuck. Doesn't it piss you off?"

"Well, yeah."

"So let's go."

They climbed over the fence. Lee fully expected whirling lights and sirens or Doberman pinschers as soon as they hit the ground. But there was nothing. From the line of trees they hid behind, they could see their destination—a gray concrete building without windows, a building that seemed surprisingly small for its purpose. "It must all be underground," Shane said.

They moved closer. The fist-sized bomb was heavy in the pocket of Lee's light jacket. His palms were sweating, and he was careful to not touch anything lest the perspiration dissolve some of the frail connections. The bomb, the most powerful one he'd ever built, would easily demolish this place. It would also take with it about a square kilometer of land. Once he had armed it, he and Shane would have about fifteen minutes to get back to the pickup and ride hell for leather away from there.

"I thought this place would be guarded," Shane whispered. "I haven't seen any alarms or anything."

"It's weird," Lee agreed.

They were nearly to the front of the building. Dead silence. Cautiously, Lee looked around the corner at the front doors. No one was there. Through the smoke-colored glass he could see what looked like a reception area. It too was empty of people. He inched toward the door, one hand clutching the bomb, ready to trigger the switch and fling it into the bushes.

Heart pounded, he put his hand to the door lever and pulled. It swung open unimpeded. Except for the faint whir of distant machinery, the room was dead.

Then he noticed how *cold* the place was, and some remote memory of a few years ago put the temperature with the sound: the fucking place was *air-conditioned*. He glanced at Shane and knew the realization had hit him also. Rage boiled up inside him, revived and hotter than ever.

They moved down a dim corridor. Behind the doors were neat, meticulous offices, all unstaffed. "I don't get it," Shane said. "Where is everybody?"

Lee flung open another door. Then felt his breath leave him. "Oh, my god."

"What?"

Lee pointed. There, lying obscenely on some major's desk, was a red-and-white box of Marlboros. *Real* Marlboros. *Cigarettes.* He reached out and touched them. They did exist. "I don't believe this," he said. He picked up the box and drew one out, ran it beneath his nose and sniffed it. He steadied himself. The cigarettes were fresh. "Want one?" he asked Shane.

Shane's eyes were glazed. "Yeah, gimme one."

Cigarettes were stuck between lips, then lit with what appeared to be a silver-plated lighter. The first draw, hesitant coughs, then deep inhaling, the nicotine filling yearning lungs. Lee expected a smoke alarm to scream out, just like in his office building, but there was none. He and Shane continued to smoke in peaceful solitude.

"Cigarettes have been illegal for years," Shane said. "Where do you think these things came from? How could they be so fresh?"

"I don't know," Lee said. He looked around quickly, then stumped out the butt of his cigarette on the major's desk. "C'mon, let's go before someone finds us."

The left the office and slid down the hall to the next door. The light came on, and this time it was Shane who said, "Oh, my god."

The room was full of refrigerators. Five or six of them. Lee pulled open one door and gaped at what he saw: the refrigerator was full of bottled Coca-Colas. "Do you believe this?"

Across the room, Shane had found a supply of ice-cold Budweiser. "Holy *shit!*"

Lee opened a Coke and looked at it, hardly believing the feel of the cold glass in his hand. He took a sip and let it play over his tongue, let the sweet cold ignite his mouth with taste, let it burn down his parched throat. Some ran from the corners of his mouth and trickled down to his sweaty chest. He stood, drinking lustily in almost orgasmic frenzy. And then the bottle was dry.

He was suddenly himself again. "Let's go. We'll leave the bomb here. I've seen all I want to." He set the explosive packet down in the middle of the floor, then moved the arming lever until he heard the reassuring click. "C'mon."

Lee caught just one glimpse of the soldier at the end of the corridor before the man screamed "Stop!"

"Shit," Shane whispered. "Oh shit, oh shit."

"You are trespassing on United States Government Property," the blue-uniformed soldier was informing them, pointing his Defense-Force-issue pistol at them.

Lee glanced behind Shane at a door marked **STAIRS**. He whispered, "How fast can you run?"

They bolted through the door, their footfalls clanging on the steel risers. "Where do we go now?" Shane hollered.

"Try to get back outside."

Above them, then could hear the soldier following. He was calling for reinforcement on his radio.

Lee burst through another door and instantly realized they were underground; there would be no doors to the outside down here.

Two more soldiers appeared in front of them. "Stop! Do not run! You are under arrest!"

"Back to the stairs!" Shane screamed.

"No!" Lee told him.

But Shane was already at the door. The shot exploded just as he touched the lever. He crumpled to the floor and lay still. The first soldier now burst through the door, tripped over Shane's body and went sprawling, his pistol landing at Lee's feet.

Lee grabbed it up and fired two shots at the soldiers at the end of the hallway, but not before a bullet ripped through his left arm. He fled for the door to the stairwell, another shot just missing him.

He raced up the stairs, his arm screaming in pain, blood already soaking his jacket. He reached the top floor and emerged into the hall, then stopped short. Two soldiers stood at the end in this way, their backs to him. Quietly, he turned and ran in the opposite direction.

His mind raced wildly, trying to figure how much time had elapsed since he had armed the bomb. Five minutes? Ten? He didn't know. He had to get out.

He turned a corner and spied an exit sign at the far end. Safe. He was safe. He reached it, fell against it, then tumbled outside.

He climbed back up to his feet, then stood in awe of what he saw. He must be behind the building. He staggered toward what his mind refused to accept, toward what his eyes could not stop looking at.

In front of him was a mountain of garbage. It stretched into infinity. He stepped across the access road and was in the middle of it. The stench was overwhelming, and he wondered why he and Shane hadn't smelled it before.

He looked around him. Refrigerators. Air conditioners. Aluminum cans. Glass bottles. Newspapers, some still tied neatly with cotton twine. Food waste supposedly being used to fertilize state farms.

He waded farther into it. His mouth, open and slack, was trying to make a sound. It was a lie, all of it. There was no Government Sanitation Program. There was no recycling plant. All of it, everything was *bullshit*. This place was nothing more than a fucking *landfill*.

The soldiers had burst outside, and now they stood watching him claw through an ocean of garbage.

Lee felt the second bullet rip into him. It tore through his shin. He cried out and sank into a pile of rotten fruit, the wetness of blood and juice and slime soaking through his shirt to his stomach and back. Now, lying face-up to the sky, he could see that the shot had come from a soldier on the roof of the building. Hate filled him, then left him as another bullet splintered his right shoulder.

Lee Houston screamed in pain, but his voice was lost in the explosion as his bomb shattered the night with the light of the sun.

(1990)

4th of July

This story was inspired by a walk with friends through our hometown on the night of July 4, 1990. I overheard a dad talking to his kids from his front door and immediately formulated a back story for him. All the fireworks going off helped, too.

Kevin stands at the front door and watches his kids playing in the driveway. They are firing Roman candles which are aimed at the stars. Kent, Kevin's oldest, is holding one of the Roman candles as it shoots. He grips it in front of him like the boys holding the flags in the parade Kevin took them all to watch this afternoon. Earlier, Kent, Melissa and Brian were catching grasshoppers and putting them in a pipe with a firecracker; when the firecracker went off, the grasshoppers would go catapulting across the yard like the circus man being shot from the cannon.

Kevin steps out onto the porch. "Don't y'all wanna wait until it gets real dark for those?"

"Aw, Dad," Kent says without looking at him.

"I'm gonna make some popcorn," Kevin says. "Who wants some?"

"Me! Me!" they all scream. The spent Roman candles are left smoking and forgotten on the gravel driveway.

* * *

Sheila, Kevin's wife, died last year. In fact, tomorrow is the anniversary of her death. He has been thinking of her constantly this week, about how she died. Ovarian cancer. There is a lot of cancer in Western Kentucky, he has noticed. She was fine one day, sitting and laughing with him and the kids at Dairy Queen on Mother's Day; a few weeks later she was dead. His mind still reels when he thinks of how fast she went.

All week he has found it difficult to concentrate on his job at the plastics factory, wondering how he would get through the holiday. But now he is grateful to have a few days off. He is surprised at how exhausted the memories of Sheila leave him.

The nights are still bad. He lies in the big bed, restless and unable to sleep. What's the matter? Why does he still feel this way?

* * *

Kent eats his popcorn like he is one of the starving children in the Sally Struthers commercials. He grabs a handful and shoves it all into his mouth. Stray kernels float to the floor.

"Pick that up," Kevin tells him. "This ain't no pig-sty."

The boy frowns but leans over and grabs up the corn, pops it into his mouth.

"Don't eat that!"

"Too late!" Melissa laughs. She covers her mouth, continuing to giggle at Kent's self-satisfied smile.

Brian is screaming for black cherry Kool-Aid, so Kevin gets up to pour everyone a glass.

"I don't like this flavor," Kent says. "I like Berry Blue."

"That stuff sucks," Melissa says. "I like Fruit Punch."

Kent turns up his nose. "That tastes like dog piss."

"Watch your mouth," Kevin says. He sets the glasses on the table. The kids grab them up and drink thirstily.

"Mom's Kool-Aid was better," Melissa says.

Outside, the sky has dimmed to a velvety purple, and fireflies are dancing among the trees in the back yard. Somewhere, firecrackers punctuate the silence.

* * *

For the past month Kevin has been seeing a girl named Kim. He met her at a club in Cedar Hill. Now Kim stays with him and the kids every weekend. At first, being so lonely after Sheila's death, he was grateful to have Kim around. But now that he and Kim are sleeping together, he feels guilty. He wonders if maybe he should break things off with Kim, at least until he gets completely over Sheila, but he doesn't know. He is confused. Maybe he is beginning to love Kim. Or maybe he just wants her physically. He doesn't know.

She comes back tomorrow for the weekend. He

wishes she would call and tell him she can't make it.

* * *

"Can we shoot the big ones now, Dad? Huh? Can we?" Kent is screaming. "It's dark enough now. Really."

"Sure."

Kent grabs the paper sack of fireworks and races through the back door to the yard. "I wanna light 'em, I wanna light 'em!"

Kevin bought the fireworks at a roadside stand on the Tennessee border. It makes him sick to think about how much money the kids are setting fire to.

First Kent sets off two Roman candles, then a whole string of firecrackers. "I wish we had some M-80s," he says in the clearing smoke. "They'd be even louder."

"You don't need anything that big," Kevin tells him. "You'd just get hurt."

After some bottle rockets and two more Roman candles, the only thing left is "The Big Finale," some twelve-dollar packet the salesman assured him would rival any professional show. "You'd better let me light this one," Kevin says. "I don't want you to burn yourself."

* * *

Kevin's best friend is Danny Powers. They have known each other since third grade. Danny moved into town in the middle of the school year and had a difficult time making friends. He and Kevin had a fight one snowy January afternoon during recess, and the next day they cut their thumbs and became blood brothers.

Danny works for the county water department. He is still single at thirty and has no children. Sometimes on long winter afternoons, Kevin thinks of Danny's freedom and is filled with burning jealousy. It's not that Kevin doesn't love his children; he only wants to be alone for a while. He only wants the opportunity to feel like an eight-year-old boy running on a playground once more.

* * *

Kevin lights the fuse of "The Big Finale." They all hold their ears as feathery spurts of fire burst forth with screeching cries. Then there is a fountain of sparks. The kids ooh and aah. Finally, blue, red and green shots spring toward the black sky and explode into huge umbrellas of color. Then everything is quiet again.

Sheila was like that—a big burst of energy that flickered and faded away, leaving a cold dark silence. Now Kevin is left, simply waiting for time to pass. Waiting. But for what?

Above, the smoke trails of the bursts still linger, floating downward like the ghostly limbs of gigantic spiders.

(1990)

A Weekend Away

"A Weekend Away" started as a dream. In fact, the dream was so vivid I woke up and immediately wrote it down. I made very few changes to the sequence of events.

I am standing in a grocery store in Louisville with my friend Dex. It is almost closing time and Dex is hastily loading my arms with tons of snacks for our all-night James Dean festival.

"I've wanted to see *Giant* for a long time," he says, snatching a large bag of puffed Cheetos.

Suddenly I freeze and point at the cash register directly in front of us. "Isn't that White Knight?" Looking closer, I can see that it is indeed Mickey

Knight, a friend from high school. We always called him "White Knight" because his hair is the lightest blond imaginable without being the color of snow.

Dex turns and squints in the direction of my stare. "Yeah, that's him. He's going to school up here now. Some technical place." He grabs a hot six-pack of Coor's. "Let's say hi to him."

"No." I put my hand on Dex's shoulder and stop him. Mickey hasn't spoken to me since the time he and his girlfriend, Kelly, caught me watching them make out on her back deck. I hide behind a cigarette rack and try not to notice Dex's sly smile. He knows I have lusted after Kelly Harvey since eleventh grade.

He laughs and claps me on the back. "C'mon, let's go."

* * *

Later, at Dex's apartment, we settle down in his sparse living room. On the television, James Dean has just been thrown out of a whorehouse. Dex leans back on the pile of pillows which serves as his couch. "James Dean was really sad. Isn't it strange how somebody who's been dead all these years can still have a following?"

"Yeah. It seems like every new generation discovers him."

"True."

"Too bad he's dead."

A couple of hours later, during the opening credits of *Rebel Without a Cause* we are both lying on our backs, our stomachs full and sore from too much popcorn, pretzels, chips and beer. Dex looks over at me. "You should move up here and go to school."

I stifle a yawn. We have discussed this many times. "You know I can't do that. I can't afford to quit my job."

He shrugs. "Get a job up here."

I turn back to the screen. "Even if I did go back to school, what would I take? What would I major in?"

"Take some writing courses."

"I don't know."

"You could live with me. It would be more fun than when we went to the U2 concert."

"Shut up and watch the movie."

* * *

The next day Dex drives us over to a park where we spend the morning hiking over well-worn and littered trails. We cross over a small brook and find an old white-clapboard chapel which has been converted into a folk-art museum. "This place is neat," Dex says as we enter through the heavy oak doors into the pristine silence.

Our steps and whispered echo insanely off the walls, amplified until I am afraid to move. Dex looks at me strangely. "What's the matter?" He looks around. "Oh, the acoustics. Great, aren't they? Some Shakers built this place. I saw a girl give a demonstration here last year. She sang some old Shaker songs. You wouldn't believe how amplified she was. Can you imagine a hundred or so people all singing in this room?"

"The Shakers must have been geniuses."

He grunts. "They couldn't have been too smart or they wouldn't have died out." He looks at me and grins. "They took a strict vow of celibacy, you know."

"Yeah. But I guess it let them channel their energy into working and inventing things."

He walks off toward the back of the room. "Just would have made me frustrated."

We climb some stairs and find ourselves in the organ loft. "The Shakers didn't use instruments," I say.

"It was added when another religious group had the chapel."

"Oh."

I sense the presence of other people. I turn and to my horror I see White Knight and Kelly. White Knight has his back to me, staring out a small window, but Kelly is facing me. She is wearing a pink sweater-dress, and I notice how it clings softly to the curves of her hips and breasts. In fact, the material is so tight I can see her nipples pointing straight out and I know she is not wearing a bra.

Suddenly she meets my gaze and a shocked half-smile comes across her lips. She gives me a quick wave and turns back to White Knight, slipping her hand inside the back pocket of his jeans. He puts his arm around her and she leans over the puts her tongue into his ear.

I turn back to Dex, who is studying an old mandolin. "Let's get out of here."

* * *

We are walking across the deserted grassy lawn of the campus of the University of Louisville. It is a fine spring day. There are scores of squirrels and birds in the tops of the high oaks. The air is still misty from yesterday's rain, but it is chilly, and I shiver in my denim jacket. "What I don't understand," I say, "is what she's doing here in Louisville."

"She's going to school at Transylvania," Dex reminds me. "I guess she came up for the weekend."

"I wish I could stop running into her. Everywhere I go, I see her. I can't even come up here without meeting her."

"I think you should just forget her."

"How can I when I keep seeing her everywhere?"

"You're obsessed, man."

"Could be."

Across the lawn, way over on the steps of Grawemeyer Hall by the statue of Rodin's *Thinker*, I can see a stooped little man in checked trousers and a bright yellow polo shirt. He waves and I hesitantly wave back. Then I recognize him, and I am frightened because I know this man is dead. "Dex, there's your grandfather."

But Dex is gone. I am alone. And the sky is getting dark. I shiver and start hurrying toward the parking lot where Dex must have gone. But the lot is completely empty.

My legs are beginning to ache. Too much walking, I suppose. But the farther I go, the harder it is to take a step, until I am no longer walking, but crawling. I am on my hands and knees, barely able to move.

A cat suddenly appears before me. Not a real cat, but the ghost of a cat I had long ago. I call to it and it trots over to rub against me. Then it runs ahead and looks back, beckoning me to follow. I am aware that it is eerily transparent.

I have followed the cat to the door of a large Victorian mansion. The cat disappears inside and I crawl after it.

I find myself in the entryway of a beautiful home lavishly furnished with first-class antiques. I climb onto a chaise lounge and lie back. The upholstery is white linen which has been painstakingly candle-wicked with flowers. It is not comfortable.

A woman I have seen somewhere before steps into the room. She is all in white with a little cap perched on her head like a paper tiara. She does not appear surprised to see me. "Wait here," she says, sounding annoyed. "Someone will help you in a moment."

Then I remember. I recall everything. I know the woman and why she seems so familiar. I know this place and how I came to be here.

Someone begins to moan. The sound grows louder until the person sounds like a banshee screaming in agony. Then I realize the sound is coming from me. I cry harder.

I have jolted myself awake. I am back in my room. My parents are sitting there watching a movie on television. I see it is the final train station scene from *East of Eden*. My father turns and catches me looking at him. "We thought you were going to sleep all day," he says.

Mom gets up and rushes over to the bed. "We've been here all afternoon. You've missed most of our visit." She smoothes my hair down. "Dr. Klein says you've made great progress. You might even get to come home soon."

I laugh, and Mom looks warily at Dad. I want to tell her what a cliché that is, how funny it all is, but I can't. I am laughing too hard. And the more I laugh, the funnier it gets.

(1989)

Katie

While shopping one Saturday morning, I witnessed a verbal exchange between a little girl and her mother, which is included basically word-for-word in the grocery scene in this narrative. As seems to be my modus operandi, I concocted an elaborate background for the two of them and a story was born. This is my favorite story out of the whole collection.

Her mother stands in the doorway, peering in at her with eyes bleary and ravaged from sleeping off the vodka she consumed last night. "What're you doin' up so early, honey? And on Saturday, too. It's only seven o'clock."

Katie puts down her pencil. "Nothing, Mama. Writing a story." She stares into the darkness behind her mother. "Did John stay over last night?"

"Yeah. Yeah, he did. So don't you make no noise to wake him up."

Katie smoothes out her Miss Piggy sheets with one hand, staring back down at her tiny, square writing on the page before her. "I won't, Mama."

Her mother smiles. "That's a good girl. What'cha writin' about?"

"A princess. A princess that has a golden canary. See, the princess is afraid to leave her room in the tower, so she sends the canary out the window every day to fly around and see things for her. Then it comes back and tells her what it's seen."

"That's real nice."

"But the best part comes when the—"

"Why don't you tell me later, honey. I need to get in the kitchen and fix some biscuits for John. He'll be mad if he gets up and they ain't ready."

"Okay, Mama." She picks up her pencil again. "Mom, can you take me over to Potter's Grocery later so I can get a new notebook? I've almost filled this one up."

"We'll see."

Katie bends over to continue her story, then stops, listening to her mother in the kitchen. Mama is kind, but she doesn't understand what books and writing mean to Katie. Mama likes watching TV, especially old movies and country music videos. Katie prefers to read. She glances over at her dresser, where *Charlotte's Web* lies on top of the box it came in yesterday. She smiles. She can't wait to start it.

She lays her paper and pencil down. Princess Emmeline will have to wait until later. Katie steps out of bed onto the cold dusty wood floor and pulls on her pink robe and house shoes, then tip-toes to the bathroom.

When she emerges, she stops outside Mama's bedroom door and, holding her breath, eases it open a crack to look at the man in Mama's bed. John lies on his back, one arm over his eyes, his hairy belly rising and falling with his breath. His black mustache curls around his mouth in a fuzzy semi-circle. She looks at his clothes piled on the floor, at the November sun glistening on his belt buckle, the one with the Mac truck on it, and she wonders if he is naked under the covers. Then, feeling a sudden, panicky guilt, she carefully shuts the door.

The living room smells of stale cigarette smoke. Kate opens the drapes and looks at the mess of beer cans and ashtrays on the coffee table. A vodka bottle lies on its side on the floor, the remainder of its contents dripping out onto the carpet. She uprights it and wipes her hand on her robe. Mama and John always make a mess after she goes to bed.

She steps into the kitchen and sits down at the table, watching Mama work up biscuit dough with a fork. "There sure is a mess in the living room," she says.

Mama continues stirring. "Well, don't worry. *You* won't have to clean it up."

"I heard you throwing up this morning in the bathroom."

"You oughta be used to it by now," Mama says, not looking up.

"I don't know why you drink that stuff if it just makes you sick."

Mama glares at her. "Look, Katie, I don't wanna

talk about it right now, okay?"

"Okay." She watches Mama drop spoonfuls of dough onto a cookie sheet and plop it into the oven. "Are you gonna marry John?"

"I don't know."

"Do you think Daddy would have liked John?"

"I don't know."

Katie pulls at a strand of her mouse-brown hair. It's oily and she'll have to wash it tonight. "When can we go get my notebook?"

"After John gets up and we eat and I clean up the house."

"Oh."

Mama glances at the clock. "It's seven-thirty. I better wake him up. I don't want him to be late for work." She leaves and Katie listens as she pads down the hall and into the bedroom and whispers, "John, you better get up." John mumbles something and Mama squeals with laughter. In a moment, she comes back into the kitchen, her cheeks glowing and a smile playing on her lips, and begins setting the table.

John follows, pulling on his shirt and stuffing it into his jeans. "Mornin', sunshine," he says to Katie, running a rough hand through her hair.

"Morning," she says.

John pours himself a cup of coffee and sits down at the table. "So, what're you gonna do today, Katie-did?"

She hates it when he calls her that. "Not too much. I got a new book to read."

"You don't wanna sit around and read a dumb old book all day, do you? Why don't you get out and play while it's still warm? Ride your bike or somethin'."

"I don't have a bike," she says. "Anyway, there's

nobody to play with around here."

"Well, then we'll get you a bike." He tugs at the sleeve of Mama's robe. "How 'bout it, Ann? Why don't you let me get Katie-did a bike?" He winks at Katie.

"I can't let you do that."

"Sure you can. Ever' kid needs a bike. How come you never got her one?"

"For one thing, I couldn't afford it. For another, she never asked for one."

"Bullshit. Ever' kid wants a bike. We'll go tomorrow and pick out a good'un."

Katie says, "John, are you gonna marry Mama?"

Behind him, Mama drops a cup and it shatters on the floor.

* * *

Outside the trees are all brown, but the sun is bright and warm. Katie watches the dead fields dance by from the dirt-streaked window of the car.

"I wish you hadn't said that this morning to John about marryin' me," Mama says.

"Why not?"

"'Cause. Men don't like marriage talk."

"Why?"

"'Cause that's just how men are. It scares 'em off. John's a good man and I don't want to lose him."

"I didn't know."

"It's okay. I know you didn't. Just don't say no more about it."

Mama pulls into the store parking lot and they get out of the car. Katie zips up her old brown jacket and suddenly feels ashamed at its grubbiness.

Inside, the store is packed with people, some beginning their holiday grocery shopping. While Mama goes toward the back for milk and bread, Katie finds the biggest notebook Potter's stocks—three hundred pages, college-ruled and everything—then chooses a new pack of American pencils.

Mama comes up behind her. "You ready?"

"Yeah."

They move to the check-out line, and Mama pulls out her foodstamp card. "Have you got enough money for that?" she asks, nodding at the notebook and pencils.

"Yes, Mama," Katie says. "I've got ten dollars."

"How'd you get that much money?"

"Saved my allowance," she says, hugging the notebook to her chest.

* * *

Back at home, Katie goes straight to her room and begins copying the story of Princess Emmeline into the new notebook, writing as neatly as she can. She finishes the story in about two hours and reads it over to herself, satisfied. She heads down the hall to show it to Mama.

Mama sits on the couch, her eyes glassy and an empty glass in her hand, watching a movie on Lifetime. The alcohol fumes are stifling. She smiles crookedly when she sees Katie. "Why don't you c'mere and talk to me, honey."

"I brought you my story to read."

Mama sets her glass on the coffee table and picks up a pack of Marlboros. "John forgot his cigarettes." She throws them back down. "Just as well. He don't need 'em no way."

"Don't you wanna read my story?"

Mama flips off the TV with the remote control and lies back on the couch. "I don't feel like readin' just now, sweetheart. I tell you what—why don't you read it to me."

"Okay." Katie sits down and reads the story carefully word for word.

"That's real good, honey," Mama says when she is through. "I hate it that the little bird died though."

"But it had to," Katie says. "Otherwise the princess would never have got the courage to go outside her tower."

Mama smiles at her. "You really have a gift, Katie. And a big imagination. I'm glad you got some brains. Maybe you won't turn out like me."

"There ain't nothing wrong with you, Mama."

"I guess I drink so much 'cause I don't have no gift like you got," Mama says. "I guess I'm just frustrated." She is beginning to drift off to sleep. "I hope you go off to college and be somebody. I want you to make somethin' of yourself."

"I will," Katie says as her mother falls asleep. She bends down and kisses her on the forehead. "I'll take care of you, Mama. You'll see."

(1988-1990)

The Bare Trees

On the drive back from visiting relatives on Christmas night in 1987 I was struck with a sudden overwhelming depression that hits sometimes when the holidays are over. I remember passing a field and seeing the bare tree limbs against the purple sky and thinking they resembled claws. Just as quickly I pictured an old man standing in that field contemplating his last days and how he would face them.

Christmas was over.

In the gray stillness of the early dawn, he raked the covers off and dragged his legs out into the chilly air and planted his gnarled feet firmly into his cold slippers. Crossing the room to the closet, he caught a glimpse of himself in the dresser mirror. He stood entranced by his reflection for some time, noticing how even his underwear, which bagged miserably around his backside, seemed old and tired. But since he wasn't wearing his glasses, the image swam before him as if he had been looking at himself in a pool and someone had stirred the water with a hand. He went on with the business of getting dressed in his coveralls.

Downstairs seemed even colder. The thermostat said seventy-five, but it felt more like fifty-five. He could never seem to get warm anymore. Most days, even in summer, he sat hunched over the gas furnace, his coat zipped up about him and his cap on his head, staring out at the sunlight which never seemed to carry its warmth in through the window panes.

He started the coffee maker, which had been his gift from his daughter last Christmas. This year she had given him a new radio (the old one had played out a month or two ago). It sat in the living room still packed in its box. She had wanted him to open it up and play it right away yesterday, but he had put her off. She was a sweet girl, but that boy she had married would have been showing him how to use it like the old man didn't have any sense.

When the coffee was done, he poured a mug of it and switched on the television, then donned his coat and cap and took his place by the heat amid the smells of Ben-Gay and stale chewing tobacco. He would sit here this way until lunch, when he would go to the kitchen, make a sandwich, drink more coffee, and return to the living room. At three he would check the mail and feed the dog. Then after Dan Rather went off at six, he would eat supper, finish the day's coffee, wash the dishes and go back to the furnace. At ten he went to bed. The only time this pattern ever changed was on the weekends. Saturday mornings he took a bath and went into town, then came home to wash clothes; Sunday mornings he went to church.

Ever since his wife had passed away in 'seventy-two, this had been his daily routine. "I worry about you, Dad," his daughter told him. "Why don't you come stay with us for a week or two? It might cheer you up." But he wouldn't hear of it. He damn sure hadn't worked all his life so he could go be a burden on his daughter. As long as he was able to care for himself, that's what he intended to do.

* * *

He awoke with a jump at three-thirty, his wife's name on his lips. He had slept through lunch. Wearily, he dug the remains of last night's supper from the refrigerator and took them out to the back porch, whistling for the dog.

It came immediately. He set down the plate of scraps, and the dog gobbled them hungrily. The poor thing was old and half-blind, more or less going through the motions as he felt he himself was. He really out to take it out to the woods and shoot it, put it out of its misery. But he knew that he never could. He needed what little warmth, what little kinship the old dog could provide him. He scratched its head. "You my buddy, ain'tcha Duke?" The dog looked at him with clouded eyes and gave a tired wag of its tail. He could tell Duke didn't have much longer.

He trudged on out to the mailbox, which was empty, and then, ignoring the pain in his legs, started out toward the big field. It hadn't snowed this Christmas, and the sky was clear and dark blue. Except for the stabbing breeze, it was a good day to walk about and get some exercise. He felt something beside him and looked down to see Duke trotting along at his heels. "Decided to join me, did ya?" he said to the dog, and it wagged its tail in reply.

Passing through the gate, he caught sight of the cedars in the fence rows and remembered what his son-in-law had said: "How come you never put up a Christmas tree?" To tell the truth, he had never been one for Christmas decorating. It all seemed a waste of time, putting all that gaudy mess up only to take it down a couple of weeks later. For the past ten years, he just simply hadn't bothered with it. Nor did he waste time worrying about gifts; he gave money and asked for nothing.

He now stood in the middle of the field, which was brown and dead with winter. His daddy had told him about the Civil War skirmish that had occurred here, and how if you looked long and hard enough you could still find buttons or garbage the soldiers had left behind. Even as a boy, he had never found a thing, though he had lived on this land for eighty years, wondering and musing about the young men who had fought and died on this small patch of earth. In the spring of 1965, the state had put up a historical marker in front of the house by the highway, telling the story of the fight, but he rarely looked at it. There were always people pulling off the road to look at it, sometimes taking pictures, sometimes knocking on the door to ask questions about the battle. He told them what he knew, no more. He didn't take to strangers, and he let them know it.

He looked across at the woods where the trees stood bare, ready to wait out the winter snow. It seemed only yesterday the new leaves had burst upon them, green with new life and expectation. Then, slowly, fall had crept into their colors, transforming the foliage into a forest of fiery orange, red and yellow. Now the leaves were dead. Everything was dead. Winter was a season of death. There was nothing he could do to stop winter any more than he could do about his own inevitable death.

But the leaves would come back in spring; he would not. There would be no spring for him this time. He felt it, surely as he felt the hard ground beneath his feet. He was in his own winter, and winter was the end.

The moon had blazed out in the darkening sky. There was a ring around it. "It'll snow tomorrow or the next day," he said to Duke. The dog watched him expectantly with its dim eyes, yellow-brown tail wagging.

He stared out across the field, concentrating on the black trees whose bare limbs seemed to claw at the deep, deep blue of the twilight sky, and the shadows in the woods that grew hazier and darker.

The wind became sharper, and he zipped his coat all the way up to the neck and stuffed his leathery hands into his pockets. "Come on, Duke," he said at last. "Let's go back to the house."

(1987)

Under an October Sky

This story has an odd history. It started life as a short story, then grew into a young adult novel which I tried unsuccessfully to get published in the late '80s. Twenty-five years later I dug it out with the intention of rewriting it. After working on it for several weeks and letting it "ferment" for a few months, I decided it worked best as originally intended—as a short story, which is presented here.

The day I found out, the Sunday afternoon Dad sat my older brother, Mark, and me down and told us, I killed a bird.

I remember the day perfectly. It was the first day of

October, that time of year when the sun shines deceivingly bright and orange, masking the cold that will soon arrive. In our part of the country, the tobacco harvest was underway, and the air was hazy with the gray, languid smoke that emanated from the barns where the farmers had started their curing fires. Being outside on a day such as that, staring out across the open fields at the blazing autumn foliage and feeling the faintest tinge of winter in the crisp air, you begin to feel as though you know what life is all about. The outdoors can make you feel more alive than just about anything, I guess.

Mark and I were out back shooting at the targets we had made from old cardboard boxes. Along with my .22, I had brought out my old Daisy BB rifle, just to see if it still worked.

"What're you doin' with that thing?" Mark asked, laughing as I carried out the back door. "Gonna shoot an elephant?"

"Fun*ny*," I said, glaring at him and turning my St. Louis Cardinals cap around backwards on my head. "I just found it in my closet. Thought I might clean it up and sell it."

Mark shrugged. "You might get a buck or two out of it."

"Thought I might see if that Hinton kid would want it."

Mark took aim at the crudely-drawn circle on the box across the yard. "Watch this, Ty." He braced himself and fired, missing the bull's-eye by about an inch. "Hell." He bent down and scrutinized his gun. "Damn sights must be off. I had it lined up perfect."

I laughed. "I think it's you that's off." I picked up the air rifle to load it and noticed Dad standing behind the screen door of the house, watching us. I sniffed the smoky air. "Can you smell it?" I called to him. "J.B. Glover's finally fired up his tobacco."

Dad was still in the doorway, the October sun on his face transforming his blond beard into a blaze of fiery red. "Can y'all come in for a minute?" he asked quietly, his eyes swollen.

Mark saw it immediately, as I did. "What's wrong, Dad?"

Dad shook his head. "Just come in for a minute. I want to talk to you."

I tightened my grip on the BB gun and followed Mark across the yard and through the back door into the dark warmth of the kitchen. The football game still droned from the TV in the den. "Miami still ahead?" I asked.

Dad looked at me but didn't answer. "Have a seat." He nodded toward the kitchen table.

"What's the matter?" Mark asked again. "Did we do somethin' wrong?"

Dad watched the floor as we sat down. "No," he said. " He reached over for his beer and took two giant gulps, then looked at us. "I don't know how to tell you this. I guess I might as well be blunt; you're not kids anymore, so I feel like I can talk to you like men."

Panic seized me. "Did somebody die?"

"No," Dad sighed. "It's nothin' like that." He looked at us. "Your mama and me are gettin' a divorce."

Mark sucked in his breath and looked away. I stared at Dad, not sure how to react. Part of me wanted to laugh; surely he was joking.

"I don't believe you," Mark croaked, and I could tell he was holding back tears.

"Please," Dad whispered. A pained expression contorted his face. "Just listen." He took a deep breath and looked down at the scuffed toes of his boots. "This is somethin' your mama and me both agreed on, so don't go blamin' either one of us. It's not anybody's fault. Not hers, not mine. Certainly not yours. It just happened."

I looked at Mark, but he was hiding his face, not wanting me to see him cry. I glanced over at Dad. He stared out the window above the sink at the washed-out gray of the old stable far across the south field, his green eyes glassy. "I'm leavin' tomorrow mornin'."

"No," Mark said, tears spilling down his face.

Dad looked back at him. "I'm sorry, son." He shoved his hands into his back pockets. "Your mama and me both think it's the best thing."

"Best for who?" I said. I suddenly realized I was crying myself.

"For all of us."

Mark sobbed into his hands. "Can we go with you? Do we have to stay here?"

"We thought it best if you stay here with your mama," Dad said.

Mark looked up and wiped his nose along his shirt sleeve, his stare angry and hurt. "Why're you doin' this? Why?"

Dad shook his head and looked back at the kitchen floor. "It's not just me, Mark. I told you." He blew out a breath. "All these years. All these years we've been tryin' to make it work. We just decided to quit foolin' ourselves."

"I don't understand," I said. "I thought you loved us."

He looked at me hard. "I do, son." He stepped toward Mark and me and knelt down in front of us. I want you two to know that. I love you both more than anything in the world."

"You're lying!" I screamed. I jumped to my feet. "That's a lie and you know it!" I ran for the outside, bursting through the screen door.

"Ty!" Dad called after me. "Ty! Come back!"

I fled blindly across the yard, across the dead, gray soil of the harvested corn field, tripping and stumbling over the hewn yellow stalks, making my way toward the woods. I finally reached them, coughing and gagging and gasping for breath. But still I ran, moving through the dense, tangled brush. Behind me, the sun was sinking quickly, casting its brilliant glow across the already vivid autumn colors, and all about me the world was fire.

I whipped off my cap and wiped my sweaty forehead on the sleeve of my faded green army jacket. Then I remembered the jacket had been my father's. I tore it off and flung it deep into the woods, out of sight. The light was fading a bit now and the darkness brought on a hushed, anxious silence broken only by a slight breeze whispering through the raspy leaves of the trees. I shivered with a sudden chill. It would be close to dark by the time I returned home, and I didn't want to be caught outside without a jacket. I turned to begin the trek back to the house. I froze.

A blackbird sat stone-like on a branch in front of me, silhouetted against the lingering amber of the twilit sky. It turned its head and squawked at me. I realized that I still held onto the BB gun. The metal barrel was ice-cold in my grip. Carefully, slowly, I lifted it. I wanted to kill the bird. I *had* to kill it. It would feel good to kill something. I took aim and fired.

The BB caught the bird's wing. It lost its balance

and fell to the ground where it sat squalling and pan-
icked, its damaged wing dangling like a freak
appendage. I fired again. The bird jumped and tried to
run. It fell, and I realized I must have hit its thigh. I
stepped closer and squinted to see it in the dim light. It
was still breathing, its eyes glassy and uncaring. It was
not making any more noise, though, and I figured that it
must be in some kind of shock. I aimed again and fired
at the bird's head, not wanting to prolong its agony any
longer. And then something happened. Something
came over me. I kept firing the gun, shooting the dead
bird again and again, making its body jump with each
shot. And when I had spent all the BBs, I jumped on
top of the mangled thing and began stomping it with my
boots until its bloody, shredded body was indistinguish-
able from the earth in the soft purple twilight.

I rushed from the woods, dropping the air rifle
somewhere among the tangle of dead vines. I emerged
into the open field and stared out at the vast scene in
front of me: the sprawling, flat farmland ringed with
woods and dotted with barns and houses; the massive,
unbounded sky, from the delicate red in the west to the
darkened east, where the moon shone bright and indif-
ferent.

Across the field, the lights of our house burned
warm and yellow. I headed for them, careful not to trip
and fall on the sharp, spear-like cornstalks I had so
recklessly flown over before. My anger was over and
now I felt spent, exhausted. The house grew as I came
closer, and I dreaded going inside, facing Dad and
Mom. I didn't know what to say to them. Dad would
probably be angry because I had run out on him, and I
certainly didn't want him mad at me right before he
left.

I paused by the back door before going in, pulling my cap down over my ears and praying I wouldn't see either of my parents. I eased open the screen door and pushed the big door back, peering cautiously behind it. The kitchen was dark and quiet. I wiped my wet eyes on my sweatshirt sleeve and stepped inside. The television still murmured toward the front of the house, and I knew Dad was probably parked right in front of it in his recliner. I tip-toed into the hall and peeked into the den. Sure enough, Dad sat watching "60 Minutes," his back to me. I passed the doorway and headed up to my room.

Midway up, I heard the door to Mom's sewing room open downstairs. I peered over the banister and watched her make her way toward the den. She stopped just inside and leaned against the doorframe. "Want some coffee?" she asked, her voice hoarse.

Dad looked around. "Yeah." He stood and flipped off the television and followed her to the kitchen.

From the stairs, I could hear cabinets opening and closing and chairs being pulled out. I sat still while the coffee brewed, listening to the silence downstairs and breathing in the heavy, wet aroma.

Someone got up and began pouring the coffee, and I heard Mom say, "I guess you told them."

"Yeah."

"How'd they take it?"

"Really hard, Ruthie. Ty was the worst. He ran off somewhere. Towards the woods, I think."

"Has he come back?"

"I don't know. I've been watchin' TV."

"That's always been your problem, Stephen," she said, her voice savage. "You were always watchin' TV or. . . somethin'."

"Don't start it again. I just can't take it anymore."

There was a long silence, and finally Mom said, "I'm sorry." Then she was sniffling. "Stephen—"

"Please don't cry anymore, Ruthie," Dad whispered. "Please." I heard his boots on the kitchen floor and the squeak of the back door as he stepped outside.

I crept up the stairs, not wanting to hear any more. I stopped outside Mark's room and knocked on the door. I didn't want to be alone.

"Go away," he said.

"It's me," I whispered.

"Go away."

I tried the door, but it was locked. "Mark. Please."

"Leave me alone, Ty. Please just go away."

I turned and headed into my room. My whole body was consumed with an awful, sinking feeling. I switched on the lamp and the first thing I saw was a picture of Dad and myself. I walked over to where it sat on my cluttered desk and stared at it. In the photograph, I was nine years old, beaming a snaggle-toothed grin from inside my bright white Little League uniform. Dad was kneeling beside me, holding me close to him and smiling open-mouthed into the camera. I slapped it off the floor and where the glass shattered.

Anxious footsteps came up the stairs and stopped outside my door. "Ty?" Mom whispered.

"I'm all right," I said.

"Can I come in?"

"Sure." I wiped at my eyes as she stepped into the room.

"What was that noise?'

"Nothing." I motioned over to the corner. "I dropped something. I'll clean it up."

"Oh." Her eyes were red and swollen, her hair

stringy. "Are you sure you're okay? Your Dad said you took it kinda hard." She leaned against the door-frame with arms crossed.

"I'm all right," I said again. Then suddenly she was sitting beside me, holding me, and we were crying together. "Why?" I asked. "Why are you doing this?"

"Because we can't live together anymore."

"Why not?"

"We just can't. We care for each other, but I don't know if we really love each other anymore."

"I just don't understand."

She drew back and looked at me. "I know you don't. You're only fifteen. We don't expect you or your brother either one to really understand."

"But don't you think we deserve an explanation?"

Mom nodded. "Of course I do. It's hard for us to put into words."

I cried silently against her shoulder. "I'm scared."

"So am I, she whispered. She stood and cupped my face in her hand. "Do you want some supper?"

"No."

"You sure? There's a pizza in the freezer."

"I'm not hungry." I lay back on the bed. "I think I'll just stay up here for awhile."

"All right," she said, opening the door. She started out and turned around. "I love you."

"Love you, too."

She gave me a thin smile and was gone.

I couldn't cry anymore. I lay among the rumpled sheets of my bed and listened to the quiet and stared at the broken picture on the floor. The glass needed to be cleaned up, but I didn't care. I knew it was possible I might step on it in the middle of the night with bare feet and run a shard of it up into my foot. Surely it would be no worse than what I was feeling now.

A sound in the back yard caught my attention. I got up and peeked through the curtains into the blackness outside.

Below me in the yard Dad was grabbing up pieces of stacked firewood and throwing them against the side of the metal tool shed. "Dammit!" he screamed. He flung another log and it dented the aluminum with a horrible bang. "Damn it all to hell!" Then he sank to his knees, crying.

I moved away from the window and switched off my light. I didn't want Dad to know I had seen him. Still in my clothes, I lay back down on my bed and stared into the darkness. I lay for what seemed like hours, not really feeling hurt or angry or scared anymore, just empty. None of it seemed real. I couldn't imagine life without Dad, and yet, here it was, staring me in the face.

"It's not happening," I said out loud in the darkness. "It's just not happening."

* * *

In the morning, just as the sun was filtering through my curtains to stir me into consciousness, voices brought me fully awake. It was Mom and Dad down in the driveway.

I leaped from my bed and peered outside. In the cold misty dawn, Mom, in her worn blue housecoat, was heading back toward the house, hugging herself for warmth. Dad leaned back against the red pickup, his hands in his back pockets, watching her walk away. He raised his eyes to my window and caught his breath when he saw me.

I don't know how long we stood there looking at each other. All I remember is thinking how cold he must be without a coat, and then remembering flinging away his army jacket the night before. He smiled at me faintly and raised his hand half-heartedly, as if trying to decide whether or not to say goodbye. I did the same. He turned to get into the truck.

I bolted out of my room and down the hall. Mark's door was still locked and I pounded on it frantically. "Wake up!" I yelled. "Mark! Wake up! Dad's leaving! Let me in!"

Mark, wearing only his underwear, finally eased the door open a crack. I shoved in past him and rushed to the window just in time to see the red pickup disappear down the road. "He's gone!" I yelled at Mark. "He's gone and you didn't even tell him goodbye."

Mark sighed and ambled back over to flop down on the bed. "Shut up and go back to sleep, Ty. It's only six o'clock, for cryin' out loud."

"But Dad—"

Mark silenced me with an icy stare. "Shut up, Ty," he said again. He turned his back to me. "He's a no-good sonvabitch."

Infuriated, I sprang over to Mark's bed and landed squarely on top of him. He made an *Ooof!* sound, and I knew I had knocked the breath out of him. "He is not!" I screamed, beating at Mark's face with my fists. Tears were suddenly filling my eyes, turning everything into a blur.

"Ty!" Mom yelled from the door of the room.

I jumped off Mark and ran to her, blinking back the tears as I clung to her. "What's wrong? What happened?" she asked me, pulling back to look at me. She glanced at Mark, who was groaning and rolling on the bed as he held his face. "What did you do to him, Mark?"

"Nothin'! He just ran in here and jumped on me!"

"That's a lie!" I hollered. I tore away from her and ran back down the hall to my room, locking the door behind me. Sobbing, I crawled up into bed and hid beneath the quilt, smothering myself with my pillow and pounding the headboard with my fists.

* * *

An hour later, when I was dressed and ready for school, I made my way downstairs to breakfast, following the scent of food like a beacon. In the kitchen I avoided looking at the head of the table where Dad usually sat and slid into my place beside Mark. He stared at his plate and ignored me. Mom, still in her housecoat, turned from the stove and gave me a small sympathetic smile. "Feelin' better?"

I nodded and took a sip of orange juice. "I guess."

She stepped over to the table with my plate and cup of coffee for herself. "Have some breakfast. You need some food in your stomach."

I picked up my fork and cut up my sausage patties. "Why do we have to go to school today? I don't feel like sitting in class."

"It'll get your mind off everything."

"Everybody's gonna know."

"Eventually."

I took a bite of scrambled eggs. "I'm embarrassed."

She sighed. "There's nothin' to be embarrassed about, Ty. People get divorced every day. It's not like we committed a crime."

"It is to me," I whispered, noticing her tense up. I looked away and took a long drink of juice.

She sipped her coffee. "I guess y'all can take the bus to school this mornin'."

Mark looked up. "How am I gonna get home?"

Mark had been driving us to school in the pickup, and then I took the bus home, rather than wait for him to get out of football practice. "Dad took the truck, and by the time practice is over, the bus'll be gone."

Mom pressed her cup to her forehead and closed her eyes. "I don't know. Can't you get a ride home with somebody?"

"Maybe Tim Rogers, but I don't know."

"Well, talk to Tim or somebody and if you can't get a ride give me a call at lunch and I'll come pick you up."

"Why can't we just take the car?"

"I'm gonna need it today."

"I don't see what for. If you'd just let us use the car I wouldn't have to worry about findin' a ride or callin' you or anything."

"For God's sake, Mark!" she exploded. "Don't you understand? I've got to look for a job! Your Dad's not gonna be around anymore. I've got to look for some way to make a livin' so we don't starve to death."

Mark looked away, silenced by her outburst. "I'm sorry," he said.

"We'd better go," I said to Mark, looking at my watch. "The bus won't stop if we're not out there."

"Yeah." He downed the rest of his orange juice and got up to grab his gym bag and his jacket. "My uniform clean?"

"Yeah. It's in the bag," Mom said quietly. She looked at me with red eyes. "You try to have a good day, okay?"

I smiled at her. "Yeah. You, too." I picked up my books from the counter, grabbed my cap, and followed Mark out into the chilly morning.

We trekked through the wet grass to the edge of the

road. I shivered in my blue button-down and blew out a puff of white breath.

"Where's your jacket?" Mark asked.

I shrugged. "I don't know. I couldn't find it." I didn't want to tell him the truth. "Mom didn't even notice I wasn't wearing it." He shook his head and looked up the road. I suddenly felt very embarrassed, thinking about the way I had jumped on him earlier. "Hey, Mark. . ."

"What?"

"I'm sorry for. . . for what happened this morning."

He nodded. "It's all right. I know." He slapped the back of my head lightly. "I didn't mean that about Dad. I was just mad." He looked down at the asphalt. "I didn't get much sleep last night."

I nodded. "Yeah."

The bus rounded the curve. "Thar she blows," Mark said.

* * *

As usual, the afternoon ride home on the bus was airless and claustrophobic, and when I stepped out onto the dusty limestone of our driveway, I felt as though the voices would continue screaming in my head forever. The bus clambered away, leaving me behind in a cold wind of exhaust fumes.

The car was gone, and I knew Mom wasn't back yet. How odd; I had never before come him to an empty house.

I knelt on the stoop and pulled out the loose brick that hid the spare key, then unlocked the door and stepped into the tomb-like living room, then moved quickly to the kitchen. I plopped my books down on the table and then leaned against the counter, unsure of what to do next.

I looked around and froze. The garbage can in the corner was filled to the brim. Trash and paper overflowed onto the floor. I moved closer and snatched up a ball of paper and began to unwad it. I stared. It was a love letter to Mom from Dad. I bent and pawed frantically through the garbage. There were more letters and even photographs. Oh, God, the photographs. Pictures everywhere. The fuzzy snapshot of Dad and Mark and me on the pier in Panama City had been ripped in half. I threw it down and dug deeper. The sixteen-by-twenty portrait of our family that had hung above the fireplace had been torn into four square sections as neatly as if it had been ripped along the side of a ruler. I sunk to my knees. All the photographs of Dad had been ripped to shreds.

Beneath the mess I felt cloth. I pulled it out. Dad's old fishing shirt. I hugged it against me and inhaled deeply—stale sweat, fish, smoke, Old Spice. . . Suddenly, I was back in a boat with Dad and Mark on Kentucky Lake. Mark had just hooked something huge. "Reel it in!" Dad was hollering. He held the net out over the opaque water. Mark was on his feet at once, rocking the little motor boat with motions that threatened to capsize us. "Sit down!" Dad roared. Instantly, he reached over the side and scooped the fish into the net—the biggest catfish I had ever seen.

And now, I dropped the blue chambray shirt and ran for the upstairs bathroom. I rummaged through drawers and cabinets. Everything of Dad's—his cologne, his razor, his toothbrush—was gone, almost as if none of it had ever been there. I rushed to Mom and Dad's bedroom and flung open his closet door. Empty hangers clanged together.

I stepped into my room. The broken glass had been

cleaned off the floor. I moved over to my trashcan. Inside, I saw what I knew I would: the photograph of Dad and me had been cut up with scissors.

I made my way back down to the kitchen garbage can. There was no other place to go. It was like a grave. I looked down and spotted an unscathed photo of Dad—probably the only one that existed now—and grabbed it. In it, he was by the trunk of the weeping willow at Grandma's, smiling broadly beneath his beard, a pack of Winstons peeking out of his shirt pocket. I smiled at it, then slipped it into my back pocket, feeling like a shoplifter.

I scooped the piles of shredded photos and letters back into the garbage. I tried to not look at the pictures; the ones I had already seen had left me with a queasy, hurt feeling. It was if Dad had been ripped away and torn to bits, leaving only minute particles of debris.

Then I remembered the jacket I had flung away so carelessly into the woods the night before. I had to get it. I had to have it again. Fast as lightning, I was on my feet and running toward the outside, toward the open field. One of the cornstalks caught my foot, and I went sprawling to the ground, hurtling toward a row of the yellow, woody things. My arm shot out just in time to save me from being impaled, and I slumped down on the hardened earth, my wrist bleeding where it had scraped against one of the stalks.

"Ty!"

I looked up. Mark was standing at the edge of the field. I threw up my hand and he started toward me. Great. I was sure I looked like an idiot.

"What're you doin'?" he asked, laughing. Then he saw my arm. "You're bleedin'!"

"I fell." My face began to burn and I realized it was

red. I stood and wiped the blood on my jeans.

"What'd you do?"

"Fell on a cornstalk."

"Damn, Ty. You better watch it. Them things are dangerous." Then he looked at me, puzzled. "What're you doin' out here?"

There was no use lying to him. "I'm going to the woods to get my jacket. I left it there last night."

He followed me as I started toward the tangled brush. "I thought you said you didn't know where it was."

"I lied." I looked back at him. "How come you're home so early?"

"Coach Brown got mad at me."

"Why?"

He watched the ground as we came to the edge of the woods. "He said I was makin' too many mistakes. He said I looked like I didn't know where my ass was." Mark laughed humorlessly. "He said if I was gonna play like that, I could just forget about playin' in the game Friday night."

"He took you out of the game?"

Mark nodded, still looking at the dirt of the field. "I tried to tell him what was goin' on, why I was playin' like I was, but he wouldn't listen, told me to just go on home. I caught a ride with Randy Harper."

"He wouldn't even let you explain?"

Mark shook his head. "Nope. The sonvabitch. I'd like to shove the ball right up his fat ass." He followed me into the maze of twisted vines and limbs. "Hey, what were you doin' out here last night, anyway?"

I glanced back at him. "Nothing. Just walking." I quickly looked away. "Watch out, there's poison ivy back here," I said, remembering that he was allergic to it.

"Hey," Mark said behind me. I turned just as he pulled the air rifle out of the thicket. "What's your BB gun doin' here?"

I shook my head. "I don't know. I guess I dropped it." I pushed on under the tree limbs until I reached the spot where I had stood last night, then glanced around in the direction I had thrown the jacket. I saw it, a smudge of green among the yellow-orange of the foliage. I stepped over and grabbed it up, my eyes starting to water. I held it up and looked at it, at the worn green cloth, at the frayed letters of the nametag. I held it against me. Now I had something of Dad's that Mom had not shredded or thrown away, something I could never let her remember that I had. "I found it," I called to Mark.

I stepped back out of the underbrush. Mark was standing still, looking at something in the dead leaves on the forest floor. "I found it," I said again, moving closer until I could see what he was staring at.

It was the bird. Only it wasn't a bird any longer, just a grotesque mass of feathers and bones and guts. It was sickening. There was no way I could let Mark know I had done it. "What is it?" I asked.

"Bird," he answered dryly. "Probably a cat or somethin' did it."

"Yeah." I pulled at his arm. "Let's get back to the house."

Mark followed behind me. "I guess you saw what was in the garbage."

"Yeah."

"It's not fair, Ty," he said. He whirled me around to look at him. "He's our *father*, dammit! What gives her the right to do that?"

I shook my head and looked down at my dusty tennis shoes. "I don't know. It's kind of scary—Mom, I mean. I've never seen her like this before."

"Not one damn thing is left, Ty," he went on. "His clothes, his stuff, and the pictures. . . the pictures! Why did she rip up all the pictures, Ty?"

All I could do was stand there, silent and open-mouthed as my brother, crying openly now, sank to his knees just as Dad had done in the back yard the night before. "It's not fair, Ty, it's just not fair!"

Silent tears flowed down my face, also. I reached into my back pocket and drew out the picture of Dad and handed it down to Mark. It took him a moment to realize what it was, with quaking hands, he took it from my fingers and stared at it. "I think it's the only one left," I said. "I found it in the garbage—Mom must not have seen it. Anyway, I took it." He stood and looked at me, his eyes glassy. "I want you to have it," I told him. "I have his jacket."

Mark reached out and engulfed me in his beefy arms, hugging me. "Thanks, Ty."

We walked on across the field toward the house, neither of us speaking until we reached the back yard. "I wonder where he is," I said.

"I don't know," Mark answered, still looking at the photo. He looked up, back toward the woods. "I wonder what he's doin', if he's thinkin' about us."

"I don't know," I said. "I hope so."

(1987)

Poetry

I never dabbled much in poetry, and there are several lines of verse that will hopefully never see the light of day. Only one of these, *October Sunday Morning*, was ever submitted for publication.

Eventide

Alone by the back door
I stand and look out at
The open countryside as the
Day dims into a deep violet sky.
Soft music floats to me from
Another room.
Although another day is
Closing, it is difficult to
Discern just when morning
Ended and evening began, as
If time does not exist
And the fragments I remember
Have been stirred into a
Marbled mixture that as a
Whole is known as
Today.
Oh, to be a child,
Innocent and barefoot,
Caring only that the days
Of summer are long and hot,
Never ceasing.
To lie on the cool boards
Of the floor and dream of
Music & Ladies & Toys & Animals
And to know that tomorrow would be
The same, predictable, boring,
Lovely day as today.
Oh, to be ignorant of
Money & Time & Expectations
& Autumn's killing frosts.

(1986)

Grey

I am empty.
At evening's fall
The purple twilight
Enters my room
And adds to my loneliness.

All day the sadness has
Hung under my eyes like
Leaded weights,
Pushing my whole expression
Down into a frown.

I have no soul to speak of.
My spirit is like
The winter trees:
Stark and bare,
No foliage to hide their nakedness.

The days all melt together—
One long stream of desolation.
They should get better,
But luck does not permit it.
So,

I feel lost,
Very much alone.
I am grey.

(1985)

Epitaph

A time-bomb.
Any minute now it will explode.
We sit upon it,
Nonchalant, arrogant,
Counting our gold while skeletons wander the desert.

We've made our place a living hell,
But we can sit in air-conditioned comfort
And laugh at it.
Nothing is wrong—why should it be?
If something's broken a new chemical will fix it.

Sweep the mistakes under the carpet.
Hide them in the attic.
No one ever goes there, thank God.
We'll say it's haunted to keep out the curious,
And if someone disobeys, it's not our fault.

Parched fields,
Strewn with the petals of long-dead flowers,
Wait for us under an electric sun,
With jutting stone reminders
Of how great we really are.

(1988)

Winter, 1978

12 years old,
Chubby-cheeked,
He stands beside his grandfather's bed,
Electric razor held awkwardly
In his small hand.

Grandpa lies on his side,
Propped up on one elbow,
His face turned up like an offering.
The sharp odor of Lectric-Shave hangs in the air
Like the green smell of fear.

Trembling razor meets ruddy skin.
Ash-gray stubble disappears with a single swipe.
Grandpa's tongue embeds itself in his cheek,
Presses flesh against metal.
The boy's hand goes back and forth,

Back and forth, until the skin
Is smooth and shiny as
A piece of red silk.
The boy stores the razor away.
Grandpa wipes his face on a towel.

Behind them, the furnace sputters and pops.
Grandpa does not thank him,
But the boy sees the
Gratitude in his grandfather's eyes.
Outside the window, the air is thick with snow.

(1990)

New Year's Day

The sky is steel gray,
The clouds riveted to the atmosphere.
Alone in my room
I sit

Fantasizing
A rock-and-roll watercolor.
I will do this all year.
So they tell me.

My mother
Is doing laundry this morning;
There will be a
Death

In the family before the year is up.
We must eat our
Black-eyed peas for lunch to insure our
Good Luck.

We have not hung our
New calendars before
Today
For fear of some

Catastrophe in the next
365 days.
So I sit by the window
With my guitar and pray for rain.

(1985)

Siren

She,
In a white, white linen dress that
Caresses her legs as
She moves like a
Silken wind,
Calls to me, laughing,
And I try to answer,
My voice lost in awe of
Her fragile beauty.

Her hair,
The sunlight shimmering upon it,
Is finely-spun threads of pure gold,
Waiting to be combed and woven by
My shaking fingers.
She dances across the sand,
Beckoning me to follow her to the water.
I reach out,
Never quite touching her.

She is always ahead of me,
A hair's breadth away
But so far.
And before I know it,
She is gone
And I am over my head,
Trying to swim among the
Tangled limbs of the dead.
Then I see her:

She,
In a white, white linen dress that

Caresses her legs as
She moves like a
Silken wind,
Calls to him, laughing,
And he tries to answer,
His voice lost in awe of
Her fragile beauty.

(1988)

Sitting

We sit on the steps,
My father and I,
Talking,
Neither acknowledging the
Long silences that fall between the
Random spurts of conversation that
Erupt like spontaneous bursts of gunfire.

He is dead.
Gray skin dangles from his neck,
Held only by dry, thread-like tendons.
"What is your favorite football team?" he asks,
His leathery tongue sliding over his scaly lips.
I tell him.
He nods and tufts of straw-like hair fall off his scalp.

I want to run,
To tear myself away,
But I am transfixed,
Frozen,
As if my feet have been
Riveted to the
Concrete sidewalk.

"It just doesn't get
Any better than this," he says
As the maggot-eaten face
Slips away and
I am left gazing at a
Bloody, wide-eyed, hideously-grinning skull.

(1988)

October Sunday Morning

Me & You
& the black cat
All piled up in the bed.
And even though the
Dead-white fog
Has not yet dissipated into
Late-morning mist,
I lie wide awake
And marvel at your sleep scent.
The soft worn quilts
Of many a winter past
Are bunched up about us,
And I shiver as I think
Of the snow yet to come.
But then you stir and
I am reminded of the
Warmth we will share.

(1986)

That Summer

At the end of May, that summer stretched before us like
a thousand glorious days.
We ran on damp grass with bare feet, raced our bikes
down Walnut to Alexander, played from yard to yard
until the hot Kentucky sun gave way to a golden full
moon and our mothers called to us from back porches
and front stoops.

Across the street, Mrs. Richmond's husband had died.
Through her lighted front windows I could see him laid
out in his casket, and an endless stream of people
coming with casseroles and kind words.
I sat on my front steps and watched them while I ate a
grape Popsicle.

The Olympics were that summer, and you could never
turn on the television without hearing those soaring
trumpets blaring the theme.
That was the summer I fell in love with Nadia Coman-
eci.   And with Sherrie down the street.
I took Sherrie to the fair downtown and she threw up on
the Tempest.

That summer was also the bicentennial, and everything
was red white and blue.
Flags were everywhere. Fireworks and parades, too.
Some college girl traveling across country painted the
fire hydrant down the street to look like Uncle Sam,
and for years you could still see his striped suit
through the rust.

That summer I took my record player to my grandmother's in the country and set it up in the big empty front room where I played Carpenters records every afternoon.

Karen's voice echoed off the hardwood floor, like she was as lost and alone as I felt.

Once there was a tiny terrarium kit in a box of Super Sugar Crisp.

I put it together and watered the tiny seeds faithfully every morning after I ate my cereal until at last the miniature sprouts appeared, filled the plastic bubble like a microscopic jungle, then withered away.

My father built a puppet theater for me that summer, and my cousin Ricky and I entertained each other with our own shows.

I made an old woman puppet from a potato and a scrap of my grandmother's dress, then forgot about it until it began to rot and smell up the whole house.

That summer I wanted more than anything to be in the movies.

I turned our house into a make-believe cinema, complete with a concession stand, a ticket booth, framed posters on the wall.

Our two bedrooms were the theaters, and I made everyone buy a ticket before they could come in.

Mamaw bought a new color TV on credit, and that summer was reruns of *The Six Million Dollar Man* and *The Bionic Woman*, *The Price Is Right* and *Match Game*, all magically new since we no longer had to watch them in black and white.

That summer was every summer.
Until we grew up. And grew old.
And then it disappeared forever.

(2008)

Juvenilia 1971-1984

It's impossible to tell how much you've grown as a writer if you can't see where you've been. This section contains work from pre-school up through my senior year of high school. I present it here as a mere oddity and not because it has any real literary value. However, these stories were necessary steps on the road to developing my craft, and I can't help but feel a bit proud of them.

The 3 Bears

I debated on whether to include this story in this collection, but since I invariably point to it as being the "starting point" of my literary career, I figured why not. My mother still has my original handwritten manuscript, complete with illustrations which I have not included here. You're welcome.

ONCE UPON A TIME, THERE LIVED 3 BEARS

ONE DAY BABY BEAR WAS TAKING

A JAR OF HONEY TO CHIPMONKS HOUSE

WHEN BABY BEAR ARRIVED AT THE HOUSE

WHEN MAMA BEAR WAS CLEANING THE
HOUSE

THEN BABY BEAR ARRIVED

WHILE CHIPMUNK WAS IN HIS HOUSE FREEZ-
ING

THEN THEIR DOG WAS IN HIS HOUSE FREEZ-
ING TO

WHILE PAPA BEAR WAS PLAYING TENNIS

THEN A LITTLE GIRL NAMED GOLDIELOCKS
WALKED IN AND ATE SOME PORRIRAGE

THEN WENT TO THE LIVING ROOM. AND SAT
DOWN IN A CHAIR

THEN IT WAS NIGHT

EVEN AT CHIPMUNKS HOUSE

THEN IT WAS MORNING

THEN WHAT A SURPRISE THE CHRISTMAS
TREE WAS UP

GOLDIELOCKS HAD PUT IT UP

BABY BEAR YELLED LOOK HE FOUND TWO
PRESENTS

(1971)

The Doll

Around 1982 I was beginning to toy with the idea of a career as a writer. I was also reading a lot of horror stories and novels. So when my tenth grade English teacher, Mrs. Johnston, gave us the assignment of writing a story, I poured everything I had into it. I used a rather unconventional narrative structure, which was a bit advanced for my age, and now seems a bit gimmicky. However, I'm proud of this story as I can see some of my later voice coming through.

Kim hadn't snooped—not really. It wasn't her fault that the nasty old cat had gotten himself locked up in the attic. All Kim had done was go upstairs to rescue him.   She had opened the door, stepped inside, and traced Kitty-Cat by his incessant mewing.   But when she had lifted him out from behind the pile of junk, the blue shoebox had fallen off the top of the stack.   Its contents had spilled, and Kim's eyes fell on the doll.

Her heart skipped a beat.   The doll was the ugliest thing she had ever seen: its clothes were torn and soiled, its face was cracked with age, and the rubber skin was peeling off.   In fact, the "skin" was held on with a straight pin on the doll's abdomen.   The painted hair had almost completely rubbed off, and the closed eyelids were missing lashes here and there.

Heart pounding, Kim set the cat outside the attic door and glanced back at the doll.   Adrenalin shot through her.   The sight of the doll was repulsive.   It looked like a dead, rotting baby in a grave.   It was not like the bright cheerful dolls Kim had in her room. They were dressed in gingham skirts or satin blouses. But this. . . this thing was all in rags.

She turned to leave, but stopped.   If her mother happened to come in here, she would think Kim had been snooping, and then Kim would get into big trouble.   She would have to put the doll back into the box and place it on the pile of junk.   But she couldn't bear the thought of touching it, and she knew why.

When she had been two, she had watched a movie on television about a woman who acquired an African doll (it was uglier than this one, but not much).   Somehow the doll came to life and chased the woman around her house.   Kim's mother said that when the little doll had run across the floor, Kim had begun screaming hysterically, and was scared for weeks afterward.

Now, standing in this dusty, dry attic, Kim looked at the doll with disgust. Heck, she thought. I'm eight years old. Who's afraid of a little doll?

She marched over to the doll and stared down into its face. Voices—

(Coward, coward!)

(Kim is a baby, Kim is a baby. . .)

(Off with her head!)

—running through her mind were drowned out only by her own thoughts: *(Looks just like a dead baby / What if it's alive/ It'll open its eyes and I'll scream and run around but I won't be able to get out just like that woman on tv / God don't let it happen / Dead baby / DEAD BABY / DEAD BABY!!!)*

Kim reached down and grabbed the doll's arm. It was soft, pliable rubber, and it gave under her fingers.

(Feels just like a real baby / Oh God / OH GOD!!)

Her mother had said dolls were more real back in her day.

(They just don't build 'em the way they usta'): her father.

Kim was trembling so badly she could hardly stand. She could feel the blood surging through her veins; could almost see them expanding, shrinking.

(Now I lay me down to sleep. . .)

She was numb. Could feel nothing. Could only watch as her arm lifted up the repulsive object grasped in her hand.

(. . . I pray the Lord my soul to keep. . .)

She fumbled for the shoebox—

(. . . If I should die before I wake. . .)

—never taking her eyes off the doll. She finally snatched the lid and brought it up to the doll.

(. . . I pray the Lord my soul to take.)

She held the doll up so that its face was only inches from her own.

"Now, dead baby," she yelled shakily, "go back in your casket!"

And with that, she started to shove the doll back into the shoebox.

But suddenly, the doll's eyes popped open. "MAMA!" it screamed.

Kim had only time to gasp before all went fuzzy, and finally black.

* * *

When she awoke in her bed, her mother was bending over her, wiping her face with a damp cloth.

"Well," her mother said, sounding relieved. "Look who's back. I must say, you gave us a fright. I found you on the attic floor—"

The image of the doll's face—

(MAMA!)

—suddenly loomed in Kim's mind. "Oh! Mom! The doll!" she stammered.

"What doll?" her mother asked.

"The doll I was holding. Where is it?"

"I don't know what you're talking about," her mother told her.

The conversation went 'round and 'round: Kim trying to explain; her mother totally confused. Finally, Kim just gave up. Her mother said goodnight and left, leaving Kim alone with her thoughts.

Her mother knew nothing of the doll, that was for certain. She had told Kim it had all been a daydream. Kim hoped so, but deep inside she knew it had been real.

She thought about the doll, upstairs in the cold dusty attic—

(If it's still up there.)

—all alone in its shoebox-coffin.   Cold.   Dead. Clawing to get out.

Kim tried to sleep, but every time she dozed off, the image of the doll's face—

(MAMA!)

—would again jump in front of her mind's eye, making her jump suddenly, heart pounding, back into consciousness.

Finally, she became so drowsy she slept anyway.

* * *

That night she dreamed she was the size of the doll. The doll was chasing her around the attic, grabbing her flesh with its cracked-rubber hands, taking the life from her body.

* * *

Kim awoke screaming in bed.   After she had caught her breath, she lay quietly, listening to the sounds of the house.   She was almost asleep, drifting into and out of consciousness, when she heard the cry.   Quietly at first, then growing louder: "Mama. . . Mama. . . Mama!. . . MAMA. . . MAMA!!!. . . MAMA!"

Kim instantly came fully awake.   She felt her heart start to pound.   Faster and faster until she thought it surely must burst out of her body.   Perspiration broke out on her face.

The cry was getting closer now, as though the doll was coming down the stairs.   But that was ridiculous.

(Is it?)

(DEAD BABY / DEAD BABY)

The cry now seemed to be coming from the hall, just outside her door.

Her whole bed was shaking with each thump of her heart, and her hair was soaking wet with sweat.

Kim glanced at her bedroom door. It hadn't been closed all the way, and a sliver of light from the hall lamp filtered through the crack, penetrating the blackness of the bedroom.

Suddenly, a small form, about a foot high, obscured a portion of the light.

(Now I lay me down to sleep. . .)

The door slowly swung open, and Kim could plainly see the outline of the doll.

"Mama!" it cried.

(. . . I pray the Lord my soul to keep. . .)

It walked slowly toward Kim's bed, until it was hidden by the footboard.

Kim wanted to scream, to run, but she couldn't. She couldn't move. Something—some force—kept her there—frozen.

(. . . If I should die before I wake. . .)

The force was overwhelming. She could only lie there as the cracked-rubber hand—

(DEAD BABY / DEAD BABY)

—closed around her ankle, and pin-sharp doll teeth bit into her leg.

(. . . I pray the Lord my soul to take.)

(1982)

Life with Mother

During my senior year of high school I started working on a novel. The humor was broad and no doubt inspired by the novels of John Irving, which I was devouring like candy at the time. In 1990 I dug it out and decided the two completed chapters would make a better short story. I'm not sure I would have been able to tolerate all those characters through an entire novel anyway.

I.
What a Life, What a Life

First of all, Mother was insane—we all knew that. Not an evil, foreboding kind but a "nice" sort. "Mother's not crazy," my older brother Beef said once. "She just. . . strange."

"Yeah," Carla, my younger sister, agreed. "She's what you call eccentristic."

"Eccent-who?" Beef asked.

"Eccentric," I corrected her.

"Whatever." Carla was not one who enjoyed being corrected. "At least we're never bored."

Mother's zaniness was the sort of thing we Pendletons knew of but never talked about. I suppose we just became used to it. Did we think it odd, for instance, when Mother decided to practice her piano at three o'clock in the morning? Not a bit. Nor when she occasionally left the dinner table to crawl around the dining room floor on all fours, mewing throatily to Dunderklumpen, our Siamese. "Just a little domestic training," she would say. There was something so oddly comforting in coming home from school to a big plate of warm zucchini-chocolate chip cookies or walking into the toilet to find a snapping turtle in the bathtub that we tended to take it for granted.

Coming from such extraordinary surroundings, we children often wondered how in the world our parents had ever married and stayed together for so long. Father seemed so *normal*. He was a respected citizen of the town, being a member of the Rotary Club and president of the local bank. He was kind. He was gentle. And he had a lunatic for a wife.

"Was Mother always so crazy?" Carla asked him one day from the front porch swing before Beef or I could stop her. Mother was busying herself in the backyard by replanting marigolds; she hadn't liked them on one side of the lawn so now she was moving them to the other side.

"Yes," Father answered without hesitation, shocking me. I had always considered not talking about Mother an unspoken rule.

"Well," Carla pressed, "how did you meet?"

We were sitting on the front porch in the cool green late May afternoon, and the smells of the outdoors brought the exciting feeling of the approaching summer—the perfume of flowers and freshly cut grass.

I sat in a lawn chair, a sweating glass of fresh iced tea in my hand. I didn't like tea, but it was one of those weeks Mother had forgotten to go to the grocery, so it was all we had in the house to drink.

Beef slouched on the edge of the porch, clad in a blue mesh tank top and a pair of gold shorts. He sat bouncing his Wilson official-size basketball between his legs, not really paying attention to much of anything, but then that was Beef's usual way. Beef was not his real name, of course—it was Ted—but the boys on the high school varsity basketball team had dubbed him that after he began to lift weights and build up his muscles. The name had stuck; our family even called him "Beef" now. In fact, it was hard to remember a time when he was ever "Ted."

At thirteen, Carla was the youngest in our family. She was also the most immature (next to Mother, of course). She prided herself on the fact that her bedroom walls were plastered with posters of everyone from George Michael to the New Kids on the Block.

She often invited her girlfriends over to try on clothes or listen to music or something and, of course, to admire her walls.

Father leaned back in his chair and scratched his chest through his white polo shirt. "The first time I saw your mother," he said, "was when we were both in the third grade. Her family moved into town from Illinois." He smiled to himself. "I'll never forget the first day she came to class. We stared at each other the whole day."

"Love at first sight," Carla commented, interrupting Father's train of thought and making him frown.

"We liked each other all through school," my father continued. "Then when we were old enough to date, I asked her out to the county fair."

"How romantic," Carla said. She kicked her legs high in the air and started the swing again. "Did you go see the hog-callin' contest and the two-headed calf? Yee-hah!"

"Shut up," I told her. "You're the one who wanted to hear this anyway."

Carla stuck her tongue out at me as Father went on. "We rode the rides and walked around mostly," he said. "Then we made the mistake of getting on the Rock-O-Planes."

"You mean them little cages that swing around up-side-down?" Beef asked, startling us all. You could never be sure if Beef was listening to a conversation or not; then when he made a comment, you jumped as if a gun had gone off.

"Yeah," Father answered him. "Exactly. Around and around and upside-down and sideways."

"Oh, no. . ." Carla said. "Did you get sick?"

"No, but your mother sure did," Father chuckled. "You see, we'd eaten all this cotton candy right before we got on the ride. I looked over at her while we were spinning and she was *green*. I said, 'Are you all right, Carol?'"

"What'd she say?" Carla asked breathlessly.

"Nothing. She opened her mouth and this big stream of pink vomit came spurting out all over me."

"Oh, my god," Beef said, letting the basketball plummet off the edge of the porch.

"She *puked* on you?" Carla cried.

"Yes," Father said, laughing. "But the car was spinning around so fast that it splashed all over her and the seats, too. Some of it even went down on the cage under us. Those people were pretty pissed off." He snickered. "So we got off, all smelly and splattered with pink puke. All those people were standing there looking at us. I felt like a damned fool. I started to apologize and your mother just burst out laughing. And then the crowd. And soon people were running over to see what the big commotion was. I guess they got a big shock when they saw us." He locked his hands together behind his head. "That's when I realized I was truly in love with your mother."

"I'm gonna be sick," Beef announced.

II.
Dinosaurs Everywhere, and Not a Drop to Drink

One afternoon in late June, Beef came home from school with his schedule for the next year. ("I'm gonna be a senior!" he would exclaim over and over again that summer.) Mother perused the computer print-out list carefully. "Woodshop again, Beef?" she asked.

"Well, it's easy," he explained. "I need the credit

and the class is easy. A breeze. I'll make you things even."

"That's okay," she told him. Even Mother knew the only thing Beef could make with his hands was a free-throw in basketball.

"Oh! I almost forgot!" he suddenly yelled, making all of us jump. "Mrs. Thompson said we would need a book for next year's English class."

"What kind of book?" Mother asked.

"I forgot," he said, looking down at his print-out, "but I know it reminds me of a dinosaur."

We all looked at each other.

"A *dinosaur*?" Carla asked. "You mean a book about dinosaurs?"

"No," said Beef, scowling. "It's an English book. Like a dictionary or something."

My mind was going crazy: *A Brontosaurus' Book of Adverbial Nouns*? *Tony the Tyrannosaurus Rex's Adjectives and Prepositions* perhaps? Or how about *A Dinosaur's Garden of Syntax*? "What exactly is this book about, Beef?" I asked finally.

"Words and stuff. I'm not really sure."

"Would you know one if you saw one?" Mother asked him.

"I think so."

"Well," she said, rising, "let's go look for one before you forget what it reminds you of as well."

* * *

To say Mother drove like the proverbial Bat Out Of Hell would be like saying Howard Hughes had a few bucks. Whipping our 1975 Pontiac from lane to lane, she would curse the other drivers loudly as she dodged around them.

"Are we going to the mall?" Carla asked as Mother

ran a red light through a scattering path of screaming pedestrians and numerous vehicles that all squealed to a stop, horns blaring.

"Yeah," Beef answered her, his knuckles white as he gripped the seat.

"Asshole!" Mother screamed as older gentleman in a light blue Lincoln tried to pull out in front of us. She swerved around him into the passing lane, almost side-swiping a bookmobile. "Damned old man! *He* shouldn't even be on the road." She snapped on the radio and country music came blasting into the car. Mother, of course, loved country music and began singing loudly with the song. "George Jones!" she informed us. Carla slumped down in the seat and stuck her fingers in her ears.

A kid in a greasy-looking t-shirt edged his old orange Mustang up beside our car at the next stop light. He grinned over at us and revved his engine.

"Look at this one," Mother said to us. "He wants to race." She roared the Pontiac's motor and popped on a huge pair of black round sunglasses that completely hid her eyes. I noticed the body of our car was rocking each time Mother floorboarded the accelerator, but I said nothing.

"What are you going to do, Mother?" Beef asked nervously.

"I'm just gonna show him who he's dealing with," she said.

"Oh, my god," Beef moaned, sinking into the floor-board.

The light turned green and we were all pinned to our seats as Mother took off, leaving the shocked Mustang Kid far behind. I looked around just in time to see him pounding his steering wheel.

"What a jerk!" Mother laughed.

"Is it over?" Beef asked as he crept slowly back on the seat, clutching his stomach. "I'm gonna be sick."

"Be real," Carla told him.

* * *

At Valley Mall, while Carla headed off toward Mu-sicVille U.S.A., I followed Mother and Beef to the bookstore. It was relatively empty, being a Thursday afternoon, so a saleswoman was upon us at once. "May I help you?"

"Yes," said Mother. "Were looking for a book that reminds Beef of a dinosaur. He needs it for school."

The lady looked at us. She blinked. "*What?*"

"Beef—"

"That's *me*," Beef interrupted.

"—needs a book for school. He doesn't remember what it's called, but it reminds him of a dinosaur."

"You mean a book about dinosaurs?" the salesclerk asked. "We have a shelf of those over in the science section."

"No," said Beef. "It's an English book—words and stuff, like a dictionary."

"Wait a minute," the woman said, holding up her hands. "Where does the dinosaur fit in?"

"Anywhere it wants to!" Mother shot, laughing and poking the other woman in the ribs. Several shoppers looked around at us.

Beef glared at her. "You're not helping," he muttered. "The name of the book *sounds* like a dinosaur," he told the saleswoman.

The lady scratched her head and frowned. "Well, I'm afraid I can't help you on that one. If it's an English book, try the reference section over there." She waved us in the direction of the side wall.

"Thank you," said Mother as she led us toward the rack of dictionaries and grammar-usage books.

Beef began to pore over every title on the shelves: *The Reader's Encyclopedia, Webster's New International Dictionary, Modern American Usage.* . . "Nothing," he said finally.

"Are you sure?" Mother asked. "Keep looking."

Suddenly, Beef screamed, "I found it!" Mother and I hurried to see. Beef held up a red paperback, a big grin spreading over his face. As soon as I saw the title, I wondered why I hadn't thought of it before—it had been so obvious. The yellow lettering across the front cover proclaimed *Roget's Thesaurus.*

"I thought a thesaurus *was* a dinosaur," Carla said later when we found her swooning over a poster of Bobby Brown in Musicville. She followed our gaze to the picture. "Isn't it great?" she said excitedly. "I can't wait to get it on my Wall of Fame."

"Well, come on," Mother said. "Pay for the damned thing so we can get the hell out of here."

On the way home, Mother took us for ice cream cones. Carla got chocolate—"to match Bobby's skin," she sighed, and Beef made gagging motions.

While we sat licking our ice creams at a stoplight in the middle of town, the roar of an engine beside us caught our attention. It was the Mustang Kid again, this time with an evil smirk on his face. The growl of the Mustang's engine was deafening. "Look who's back," I said.

"I think he's mad," Beef commented.

"Sore loser!" Carla yelled at the Mustang Kid through her open window. The Kid replied with an angry rev of his engine. "Gee!" Carla exclaimed.

"Back for more, huh?" Mother said.

"Oh, no, not again," Beef mumbled as he made his way to the solace of the floorboard.

The Mustang Kid was watching us, grinning eerily. "He's crazy," I said as he and Mother eyed each other with all the rancor of two dogs about to rumble.

The light turned green.

Mother and the Mustang Kid took off simultaneously. Carla, who had been eating contentedly, was thrown back against her seat, her ice cream mashed against her nose and forehead. "*Gugg!*" she exclaimed.

Mother was howling with delight—we were passing the Mustang Kid again!

A puff of white smoke exploded from the front of our car. "*Merde!*" Mother cried. She slammed on the brakes and pulled over to the shoulder of the four-lane boulevard. The impact shoved Carla's face into her ice cream once again.

"Oh, god, oh god," Beef was moaning.

"Shut up!" Mother screamed.

"My ice cream!" Carla wailed.

The Mustang Kid flew past us through the fog of smoke, his horn blaring triumphantly.

"Jeez," I managed to say.

* * *

Father also said "Jeez" when Mother called him later from the garage. I heard him scream it plainly even though Mother was across the room with the receiver pressed tightly against her ear.

Carla, still with melted chocolate ice cream on her face, went to borrow the key to the ladies' room so she could wash off. When she returned, the four of us sat in the service station's office in silence while we listened to the mechanics clinking and tinkering with our car out in the garage. Beef borrowed a dime from Carla and bought a stale gumball from a machine in the corner. He walked around the office chomping and popping and blowing bubbles until Mother told him to sit down and be quiet. I sat on the old car seat that had been turned into a sofa and played with a cigarette butt on the grimy tiled floor with the toe of my tennis shoe. Carla announced that she was worried one of the mechanics might steal her Bobby Brown poster. "Shut up, Carla," Mother told her. "Just shut up."

When we were finally home a few hours later, Father was already there. We found him sitting in the dark at the kitchen table, a glazed expression on his face as he watched us file in. Wordlessly, he handed Mother an envelope.

She tore it open and quickly scanned the letter inside. Her face brightened. "Yee-*hah!*" she squealed, reminding me of Carla that day on the porch.

"Oh god," Father said. "What is it?"

"You'll never guess."

"Do I want to know?"

"My whole family is coming down for the Fourth of July!"

"Oh god," Father said. He tried to rise from his chair but fell back, his face completely drained of color. "The whole family?"

"Yes!" Mother said. "My mother, Aunt Bertha, and Sally and Fred and their kids."

"Oh god," I mumbled. Aunt Sally and Uncle Fred's children, Kelly and Alex, were holy terrors. The last time they had visited us they had broken down the banister on the stairs and jumped on my bed until the frame exploded and sent them plummeting to the floor. And Aunt Bertha lived with them now; she chewed tobacco.

"Oh, isn't it wonderful!" Mother exclaimed. "My

whole family!"

"Oh god," I repeated.

"Jeez," said Father.

III
Family Reunion

"There they are!" Mother screamed as an old dusty blue station wagon pulled into the drive.

"Oh god," Carla muttered as she crouched in a corner of the living room.

I stepped up behind Mother at the door just in time to see Grandmother racing across the lawn. "Carol!"

"Mother!"

The two of them caught each other and hugged. "Kissy, kissy, kissy!" they said in unison.

Behind them, Great Aunt Bertha was hauling her rotund frame from the front seat. She wore a hideously bright green sack dress with a shocking pink flower print. A tiny straw hat sat on her head like a dead cat; red plastic roses bloomed from the weaving. "Martha!" she grunted at Grandmother. "Least you could do's help me the hell outa this damned car!" She looked around behind her. "Fred!"

"Yo, Bertha!" Uncle Fred called from where he struggled with three heavy suitcases at the back of the car.

"Be careful with my bag! I hear you clunkin' around back there."

"Sorry."

A large black Labrador bounded out of the station wagon and over to the nearest tree to relieve himself. "Rufus!" Uncle Fred screamed at the dog. "Git yer ass over here!" The dog finished his job and trotted back over beside Uncle Fred. He plopped down and proceeded to lick his balls.

"They brought a dog," I said to no one in particular, trying to make myself believe it. Dunderklumpen wouldn't like this at all.

"Are we finally here?" a young girl's voice cut across the yard.

"Thank God," a boy said. "I gotta take a leak."

Kelly and Alex. I felt panic welling up in my stomach already. They and Aunt Sally stood on the lawn. "I've always loved this house," Aunt Sally whispered.

"It's not so great," Kelly said.

"I just wanna get to the john," Alex said.

Mother hollered for Beef and me. "Come out here and help Fred with their stuff."

I made my appearance as Beef stumbled around the side of the house, basketball in hand as usual. Rufus bounded over to us and began licking at us frantically. "Down!" Aunt Sally yelled. Rufus slunk back to the car.

Grandmother was upon us at once. "Oh! They've grown so much!" She grabbed Beef's shoulders and squeezed them affectionately. "Ted! You're so big and strong now! Give your grandma a big hug!" Beef stooped to embrace her and she gave him a loud, wet smooch on his cheek.

"We call him Beef now, because of his muscles," Mother said.

"Beef!" Grandmother giggled. Then she looked over at me. "Boy, you've just grown up all over the place." Whatever that meant. She pinched and hugged and kissed to her fill.

"Carla's inside," I told her.

She started off toward the house. "I do so want to see the little dear."

Alex ran up to us. "Hey, cousins," he said. "Like to talk but I gotta piss real bad. Where's your can?"

"Go on in," I said, motioning over my shoulder with my thumb. "First door on the right."

"Great. See ya later, okay?"

"Sure." Beef and I looked at each other.

Aunt Sally was chatting with us about the long drive. Kelly pulled uncomfortably at the crotch of her yellow jogging shorts. Bertha bit off a plug of chewing tobacco and began chomping hungrily, spitting her juice at a nearby dandelion.

Uncle Fred loaded us up with two heavy suitcases each and followed us into the house to the guest room. Uncle Fred wore a duck-billed cap to church and associated every NFL game with a six-pack of Budweiser. His southern drawl sometimes made him difficult to understand. "Whur we sleepin'?" he asked as we huffed and puffed with the bags up the stairs.

"What?" Beef said.

"You know, where's ahr rooms?"

"You and Aunt Sally have one guest room," I told him, "and Grandmother and Aunt Bertha have the other. Kelly and Alex are doubling up with Carla and me."

Fred seemed relieved to find he and Aunt Sally were at the opposite end of the hall from Grandmother and Aunt Bertha. "Bertha farts in her sleep," he said.

Beef snickered through his nose and quickly covered it with a fake coughing fit. I managed to keep from laughing by biting my tongue; I bit too hard and my eyes began to water.

"*Pphht! Pphht! Pphht!* I hear it all night long. Keeps me up for ahrs."

"That's too bad," I said.

"Fart, fart, fart," he muttered, stomping around the guest room, his beer belly jiggling like Jell-O.

Mother's voice filtered up from downstairs. "I see you brought Rufus."

"Yes, I hope you don't mind," Aunt Sally said as Beef and I descended the stairs. "You can't imagine what we went through with that dog in the car."

"Oh. . . did he get playful?"

"Worse than that," Aunt Sally told her. She lowered her voice to a whisper: "He shat on Bertha's Sunday shoes."

"Damn dog," Aunt Bertha muttered from the chair she had set up housekeeping in. Already a pile of junk had started to form around her: crossword puzzle books, a Frederick's of Hollywood catalog, a box of tissues, a bag of chocolate crèmes, and a foam spit cup.

"Let's get outa here," Beef whispered to me.

* * *

Outside, Beef grabbed his basketball and challenged me to game of horse. "So what do you think about Alex?" he asked, shooting and missing the basket.

"That's an 'H,'" I said about the missed shot and "I don't know" about Alex.

"Yeah," Beef said, passing the ball to me. "I feel sorry for you, having to sleep in the same room with him."

"It shouldn't be that bad," I said, shooting the ball. It sailed cleanly through the net. I shot again, missing.

"'H,'" Beef said. "You'd better hope he ain't a bed-wetter or somethin'."

I glared at him. "I doubt that. But if he is, *you* can have him."

Beef laughed and threw the ball at the goal. It

bounced off and back toward the house, almost hitting Carla as she slunk through the back door. "Watch it!" she cried.

"Jeez!" Beef said. "Who pissed in your Wheaties?"

"This is gonna be a long week," she said, ignoring him. "Kelly thinks U2 is some kind of nuclear weapon and George Michael is a wrestler."

"Oh, horrors," I said.

"Shut up," she snapped.

"Here they all are," Mother said behind us through the screen door. We looked up. "You kids get in here and be sociable," she told us.

We looked at each other and made our way inside to the family room. We sat on the floor by our cousins. They glared at us and we glared at them as the adults led the conversation. Father and Uncle Fred discussed the baseball strike while Aunt Bertha listened intently, nodding her greasy brown head and spitting tobacco juice into her cup with a *hhooocckkk—ptui!* that made my flesh crawl.

"I've been giving Carla piano lessons," Mother said. "She's really good—almost better than I am."

"Play something for us, Carla," Grandmother urged.

"Oh, yes, do," Aunt Sally chimed it.

Reluctantly, Carla made her way over to our Baldwin, sat down on the bench and rummaged through the huge pile of music books until she found what she wanted. "I'll do my recital piece," she said, and her delicate fingers began the first soft notes of *Clair de lune*. When she was finished, she slid off the bench and gave a slight red-faced bow.

"Boy, that girl can really play!" Grandmother screeched over the family's thunderous applause.

"I made a few mistakes," Carla said.

"Well, I didn't hear them," Aunt Sally said, still clapping.

Mother sighed. "Well, after that little concert, I'm just about starved. What about dinner? We're grilling hamburgers."

"I feel like having one of your big salads," Grandmother said.

A look of horror froze Mother's face. Her mouth dropped open.

"What is it, Carol?" asked Aunt Sally.

Mother closed her mouth and swallowed. "I forgot to get lettuce."

"Oh, Carol," Grandmother moaned. "How in the hell do you expect to fix a salad with no lettuce? You know I can't eat red meat."

"Why don't we all just go out for dinner?" Father said.

"Oh, yes!" Mother cried. "There's the best little restaurant on the other side of town. It's this little log cabin where they let you cook your own steak. And they have a huge salad bar."

"That sounds like fun," Aunt Sally said.

Aunt Bertha grunted. "If I pay for a meal, I expect somebody else to cook it for me."

"We'll buy yours," Father said.

Bertha nodded. "I'll get my hat."

IV
The End of It

To tell the truth, the last thing I wanted to do was go out in public with that crew—especially to a restaurant where everyone knew me. I pulled Mother aside and feigned a sick stomach. "I'll have Pepto-Bismol for dinner," I said.

She nodded. "Add it to a strawberry milkshake."

And it appeared that Alex didn't care too much for the idea of going out to dinner, either. "Do I have to go?" he whined to Aunt Sally.

"Alex can stay here, too," Mother said.

Great. Let's hear it for Mother.

So Alex and I watched the others pile into Fred and Sally's station wagon. Alex turned from the front window. He was grinning. "Know what we oughta do?"

"What?" My head was filled with visions of emptying boxes of soap into the neighbors' pool and contests to see who could be the first to tear down the house with his bare hands.

"Let's get drunk," he suggested.

"I think not."

"What about girls?" he asked.

"What about them?"

"Can you get some?" There was an odd gleam in his eyes. I didn't like it. He looked like Dracula at a blood bank.

"How old are you?" I asked.

"Twelve."

"I don't know any girls who would be interested in a twelve-year-old." I leaned back on the sofa, my hands behind my head. "Why don't we just order a pizza?"

He shrugged. "Okay."

* * *

I was on my fourth piece of take-out pizza (Alex's favorite—meatballs, tuna fish and anchovies) when we heard the car doors outside. We looked up from where we sat in the living room floor as Mother came in the front door, a bandage on her forehead. She was followed by the others, and they were all grubby and disheveled.

"Get your stuff together, Alex," Aunt Sally said. "We're leaving."

Alex was frozen with a slice of pizza halfway between the box and his open mouth. "Why?"

"Jus' *do it!*" Uncle Fred bellowed.

Alex looked at me, shrugged, dropped his pizza and headed for the upstairs.

Bertha waddled past me. "I don't believe this shit," she said. "Fred and Sally drag me all the way out here for a damn fire."

"Fire?" I said, looking at Father as he shuffled in. "What happened?"

Father sighed. "Your mother tried to do her fire-eating act at the restaurant and caught the curtains on fire. She tried to put out the blaze with her steak and hit an older man over the head with it. The place turned into a free-for-all inferno, people flogging each other with their dinner while they tried to get out."

"Was anyone hurt?" I asked.

"Just your mother." He motioned to where she sat sullen in the recliner. "She got knocked unconscious with some old woman's leg of lamb."

I stared at him, then at Mother, then at Beef and Carla who were just coming in. "So the restaurant," I said, "is it. . . "

"Gone," said Beef.

"Burned to the ground," Carla said.

"But why are you leaving?" I asked Grandmother.

"*Her!*" Grandmother screeched, pointing at Mother. "She needs to be locked up somewhere." She stormed off upstairs.

"I was only trying to be funny," Mother said in a small voice. She clutched her head in pain.

"Ha ha," Father said.

The relatives were gone two hours later. Fred even squealed his tires as he took off. Father watched from the front window as the station wagon's tail lights disappeared. "Well," he said, "at least one good thing came of all this."

But as the days went by, something strange happened. Mother began acting. . . *normal*. No longer did she announce she had taken up fascinating and exotic hobbies (like her once-beloved flamenco dancing). No longer did she talk back to the television, telling Johnny Carson that his tie looked like one Desi Arnaz wore once on *I Love Lucy*.

Now, Mother fixed normal dinners, did normal housework, involved herself in normal activities. She even talked of doing volunteer work with the elderly. We were amazed—now our mother was like everyone else's.

We loved the new Mother, but at times we missed the old one. Our household settled down. It was comfortable but boring. No longer did we have Mother to entertain us twenty-four hours a day. We had to make our own fun. And the novelty of a normal, regular routine soon seemed monotonous.

Still, as Beef would say years later, "Thank God for leg of lamb."

Amen.

(1984-1990)

About the Author

Will Overby writes books for kids, adults and teens. He and his wife have two grown children. They share their Kentucky home with three neurotic cats and an obsessive-compulsive dog. Connect with him at his website, *willoverby.com* or find him on Twitter, *@Will_Overby.*